FIELD-TRIPPED

Ad Agency Series, Book Three

NICOLE ARCHER

LITTLE DIXIE REGIONAL LIBRARIES
111 N 4th STREET
MOBERLY, MISSOURI 65270

Twist Idea Lab

Field-Tripped Copyright ©2017 by Nicole Archer

ISBN:978-1979439183

First Edition

All rights reserved. No part of this publication may be reproduced, distributed or transmitted in any form or by any means, including photocopying, recording, or other electronic or mechanical methods, without the prior written permission of the publisher, except in the case of brief quotations embodied in critical reviews and certain other noncommercial uses permitted by copyright law. For permission requests, write to the publisher:

> Twist Idea Lab, LLC
> 707 Parkview Circle
> Richardson, TX 75080

This is a work of fiction. Names, characters, places, and incidents are a product of the author's imagination. Locales and public names are sometimes used for atmospheric purposes. Any resemblance to actual people, living or dead, or to businesses, companies, events, institutions, or locales is completely coincidental.

Field-Tripped Soundtrack

This book comes with its own soundtrack. If you're reading on a device with Internet access, simply click the link at the beginning of each scene. If you don't already have a **Spotify** account, you'll need to sign up for the free streaming service. You can play it online or from your mobile device.

If you're reading a print version or have a device without Internet access, you can find the **Field-Tripped** soundtrack on my **website, nicolearcher.com**, as well as on **Spotify.com** under user name: **nicolearcherauthor**.

"Be free of attachment to the good experiences, and free of aversion to the negative ones."

— Sogyal Rinpoche, The Tibetan Book of Living and Dying

ONE

Eli Is A Chill Motherfucker

"No matter how fast you flee, there are times when pain catches up with you. And in between those times, life is so boring you could scream." — Henepola Gunaratana, Mindfulness in Plain English

---

Eli's Mixtape: Gorillaz, "Clint Eastwood"

MANHATTAN, NEW YORK

My new goal is to be as unsuccessful as possible. So far, I'm crushing it.

Women, furniture, music, stuff, and stress—I've given it all up for good. I've even started meditating. I'm doing it right now.

Do nothing, Eli. Be nothing. Remove all distractions. Clear your mind. Think peaceful thoughts. Omm.

This is way better than seeing a shrink. What's the point of rehashing memories for two hundred bucks an hour? If I felt like talking about my past, I would have done it a long time ago.

Meditation is the way to go.

Before simplifying my life, I spent forty hours a week slumped over a computer at Shimura Advertising, where I'm a graphic designer. On the weekends, I DJ'ed at clubs until the wee hours of the morning. The rest of the time I produced music for the DJ community.

I don't even want to get into how many hours I wasted sleeping with women who wanted too much.

At some point, I was bound to crack. And nothing says it's time to take a mental health break like freaking out in the middle of a set, packing up your turntables, and leaving hundreds of sweaty club-goers in stunned silence on the dance floor.

I thought I saw my ex that night.

There was also that time I lost my mind on a coffee barista.

Every night, I'd fall asleep, wondering what happened to my life. I used to be an athlete. I was a snowboard racer and almost went to the Olympics. But that's another story. You can watch old ESPN footage of *Eli St. James's Fall From Grace* on YouTube.

The point is—success doesn't matter. It's just a word. Life can change in a heartbeat. Everything can be taken away. But if you don't have anything, there's nothing to take. No attachments, no problem.

Simplicity is the key to happiness. So is meditation.

This cushion is like sitting on a rock. I would give my left nut for a leather sofa and a big-screen TV right now. What was I thinking, getting rid of my stuff?

See? That's attachment talking. Buddha said attachment leads to suffering.

I got that from my $5.99 Buddhist quote-of-the-day app. I'm very attached to that app.

Anyway, Buddhism is the way to go. I'm simplifying my life. I'm done with difficult. I'm no longer a slave to being busy.

Now I'm Henry David Thoreau on Walden Pond.

Except in reality, I'm Eli St. James, who lives in a shithole Manhattan studio with no earthly possessions.

But I have more time to exercise and sleep, and I'm a lot less stressed. I still work at the agency, because it's easy and creative, and then I leave and do a whole lot of nothing.

So what if I'm mind-numbingly bored? It's good for me.

Isn't it?

I open one eye and see a cockroach scurrying across the floor. It's the most exciting thing I've seen all week. I jump up and stomp on it.

After that, I walk to my job at Shimura Advertising. Slowly. Because I'm a chill motherfucker who meditates.

SHIMURA ADVERTISING AGENCY, NEW YORK

If I had anything on my desk right now, I'd sweep it off. "No, never. No fucking way am I going to Colorado!"

I'm in the middle of a staredown with my boss, Skip. He took over Shimura Advertising after his dad died. He's kind of a joke of a boss. Most of us don't take him seriously. But I'm taking him seriously right now.

"You are aware that I'm the one paying your salary?" His unblinking black eyes are just barely visible under his squint.

I lift my chin. "Sorry, can't help you out on this pitch."

"You're fired."

I snort. "What?"

"You heard me. Pack up your shit." Skip covers his mouth. "Oh, oops, you don't have any shit. You gave it all away. Well, that should make it easier." He spins on his leather boots and stomps away, head held high.

I'll wait for five minutes. He'll be back, begging me not to quit.

Ten minutes pass.

I turn on my computer and check my email. Nothing from Skip. But he'll be back.

Four more minutes pass.

I check my savings account. I could get by for six months. A year, maybe. And do what? This requires serious planning. I have heart palpitations. And is that sweat on my upper lip? *Jesus.* I'm relapsing.

I may be chill, but not when it comes to Colorado. When I left home, it was for good. I cannot go there. She's there. Everyone died there. *I* died there.

Just before I'm ready to drop to the floor and meditate, Skip zips down the office slide and lands two feet away from my cubicle. "Ready to pack up your toothbrush and go boardin'?"

"No." I spell it out in case he didn't hear it the first time. "N. O."

He sighs and sits in my office chair. "All right, what's it going to take, St. James? I thought you'd be leaping in the air, Cirque-de-Soleil style. This is such a cool opportunity. Proton Sports. Adult winter camp. So much fun." Skip's tone is anything but fun. "I thought you grew up there. What's the problemo? I was serious, by the way. If you can't go, I'm going to have to can you."

I pinch the bridge of my nose to stave off impending hyperventilation. "Where is this camp?"

"Breckenridge. You're not filling me with false hope by asking, are you?"

There's no way in hell I'd run into her in Breckenridge. I could just fly in, fly out, and get it done with.

What am I thinking? I can't go back!

I'm thinking I need a job.

Skip hangs his head. "Look, I'm going to be frank with you. You're not the only one I'll have to lay off if we don't get this business. I'm sure you've noticed the lack of billable hours around here. Think about our dear copywriter, poor single mom Avery. Think about all the families that Santa Claus will skip, if they don't have a job. You really want me to be that kind of Grinch?"

"Is this a guilt trip?"

"Is it working? I thought you were a compassionate Buddhist now?"

This compassionate Buddhist is seriously thinking about kicking his boss's ass. "How long?"

"Two weeks total. You'll be in and out before the holidays. Lickety-split." He dices his hand through the air.

"Who else is going?"

"You—I hope—me, Avery, Sabrina—"

"Sabrina! Hell, no." I "dated" Sabrina a while ago. She's an account manager here at the agency. She's also a stage-nineteen clinger. Case in point: she's been hanging onto our non-relationship for a year past the sell date. Her *Sports-Illustrated*-swimsuit-model attractiveness morphed into Britney-Spears-shaved-head ugliness a few too many times.

She was a master at the mind fuck. And I hate games. Plus, she's high maintenance, and I'm as low-maintenance as you can get without being dead.

Except right now. Right now I am not low maintenance. I am high maintenance. Very high.

Adding her to the mix makes this situation even worse.

"I need the whole team," he says. "That's the only way we're allowed on this pitch."

"Who else is going?"

"The intern. Because she's free. Fischer, the new developer. And"—he sticks his tongue out and rolls his eyes—"Jerry."

"I thought you hated that guy?"

"I do. But he played hockey in college, and I need all the wintery skills I can get. Including yours." He clasps his hands in prayer. "Pretty please, St. James, with a bonus-if-we-win-this-account sprinkled on top? I need you. Don't make me beg."

"Isn't that what you're doing right now?"

"Yeah, but I'll get down on my knees, which is huge, because I'm wearing nine-hundred-dollar jeans."

I can't believe I'm about to say this next sentence. Maybe I should see a shrink after all. "Okay, but you owe me."

"No, I don't. What about all that time off I gave you when you were moonlighting at your second job?"

"I didn't take time off to DJ."

"Okay, what about turning a blind eye when you were screwing Sabrina?"

"Is that against the law?"

His left eye twitches. "Just get your ass in the conference room, St. James."

It's an inferno inside the conference room. The coworkers accompanying me on this horrible journey are already seated at the table.

Sabrina's gaze follows me like one of those creepy paintings in a haunted house. "Are you going?"

"Looks like it," I grumble.

Preeti, our Indian intern, hooks up her laptop, and a chart pops up on the overhead screen.

Skip pulls out a laser pen and shines a red dot at the chart. "Okay, team, let's discuss our upcoming team-bonding trip."

Team bonding trip, my ass. This is extortion.

Our copywriter, Avery Adams, is firing ocular missiles at our boss. Normally, she's sweet and silly and reminds me of a voluptuous version of Audrey Hepburn in *Breakfast at Tiffany's*. But right now, she's glaring at Skip like he's Sigourney Weaver and she's the alien.

"How many times do I have to tell you? I can't go! Who will take care of Austin?" Austin is her little boy. She had him by herself with a sperm donor.

Skip shines a red dot on her forehead. "Proton has a guy at the resort who will watch your kid when you're busy."

She swats the dot away. "You expect me to leave my kid with a strange man? Are you insane?"

"What's there to do? Feed him. Play with him. What could go wrong?"

"Isn't Breckenridge where that cannibal guy lived?" asks Sam, the developer.

"Shht!" Skip zips his lips. "Nobody asked you, Fischer."

Avery dials up an expression similar to a serial killer. "I will kill you in your sleep if something happens to Austin."

Skip sits on the corner of the table and folds his arms across his chest like he's the most important person in the room.

Newsflash: he's not.

"Listen up, team. In case I wasn't clear: you don't do this pitch, you're out of here. I've been beyond chill with all your little personal problems." He flutters his hands like birds in flight. "Your kid problems. Your relationship problems. Your second careers..." He directs the last two items at me. "Now you need to do me a solid and do your jobs. Or I'll find someone who can. Besides, it'll be fun. Two weeks in colorful Colorado. What's not to love? Fresh air. Parties. We'll do a little schussing down the slopes." He swooshes his arms like he's cruising down the mountain. "Then we'll win the business and come home. Consider it a paid vacation."

"I'm down," Sam says.

"I am not down," Preeti says. "I have a restaurant job."

"I'll pay you out of my clothing allowance," Skip says.

"How much?"

"More than you get paid at your waitressing gig. Are we done, yet? Can I get back to my employees now? Thanks. As I was saying before I was so rudely interrupted... The intern—"

"Preeti," says the intern.

"The *intern* placed your wintery skills next to your name."

"Was that what that survey was about?" That question came from Jerry Reno.

"Shut it, Jerry," Skip barks.

Jerry, who is two hundred and twenty-five pounds of steroid-plumped muscle, shrinks back in his seat. He's our finance guy and also a dead-ringer for a *Jersey Shore* cast member.

I point to the screen. "Next to my name it says 'tons of outdoorsy shit.' What exactly is that?"

Skip shines the red laser in my eye. "Weren't you on the Olympic snowboard team, St. James?"

"No, I blew out my knee." This is a story I don't care to rehash in front of my coworkers.

"What's it been? A decade? I'm sure it's good as new. And bonus, you grew up in Colorado. Plus, you have that beard. Instant Brawny Man." He winks and shines the light on the next employee.

I pinch my lips together, before I say something that lacks serious compassion.

Sabrina interjects. "I, like, don't have any wintery skills." She snaps her gum twice then continues. "I grew up in Florida."

Skip beams the red dot next to her name. "Says here you're an avid jet skier and wake-boarder?"

Her head tilts like a puppy trying to decipher human words.

"Just pretend you're on the water when you're on that fresh pow-pow, and we're golden."

That is the most ridiculous thing Skip has ever uttered. But coming to Sabrina's defense would give her too many ideas—like I might want to sleep with her again. Which I don't.

"What's up with the big blank next to Fischer's wintery skills?" Skip turns to Preeti. "Am I going to have to dock your pay?"

"You don't pay me. And Sam was in the military. Afghanistan, correct?"

Sam clenches his fists and rolls his neck. He's a live wire, that one. And sketchy. There's something off about him. Take his ink, for example. I have sleeves of my own, but mine are all peaceful and harmonious. Sam's are all about death and destruction and skulls and blood. Super disturbing.

That said, he's a fricking genius with code. He can build anything. And hack anything. I worked with him on a web project, and he broke into my computer one day when I was at lunch, claiming I didn't give him the right files. I was furious. He claimed my password is too easy. After that, I changed it to *Fischerisafuckingasshole.*

Skip rubs his hands together like Mr. Burns on *The Simpsons.* "Excellent, Fischer. You can build booby traps for the other team and bury land mines and shit like that." He turns to Preeti. "What about you, intern? Where are your wintery skills?"

She stuffs a pencil in her tight black bun. "I'm from southern India."

"Can't you do anything besides crunch numbers?"

"I was the captain of my field hockey team."

"Hmm." Skip rubs his chin like he's trying to imagine our uptight MBA candidate sprinting down a field. Then he stands and waltzes to the door. "I've got a meeting with our hot PR chick. She's steering the ship while I'm in Colorado. Okay, kids, brainstorm away. I want wintery magical ad concepts before we leave on Friday."

Instead, we stare at the chart without speaking.

Avery moans.

My phone vibrates with a notification from my quote-of-the-day app. *"Do not dwell in the past, do not dream of the future, concentrate the mind on the present moment."*

Holy shit, it's like Buddha himself is watching this scene unfold.

Fine. That's exactly what I'll do. Concentrate on the present. This is just an ordinary business trip. No big deal. So what if it happens to be in that horrible place? Wherever you go, there you are.

Except right now. Right now, I'm in hell.

TWO

Charlie Is Dog Tired

Eli's Mixtape: Gyft, "They Just Don't Know"

ORION AGENCY, DENVER, COLORADO

THAT ICKY VOICE POPS UP. *It's Monday. You're still at work at 10:00 p.m., and now you're hunting for dick. You need help, Charlotte.*

I ignore my inner nag and swipe right on two guys. Hopefully, they'll message me back tonight.

Not that I can get down and dirty, with my shoulder. Two weeks ago, I dislocated it hang gliding. Normally it doesn't bother me that much, but I've spent all day in front of my computer, putting the final touches on my campaign for the pitch next week, and now it has its own heartbeat.

My border collie, Julius Seizure, paws my leg. I lay on the floor with him and pet his furry belly. That's what I love about owning my own ad agency; I get to bring my dogs to work.

L.L. Drool J, my St. Bernard, scoots over and licks my hand. My three-legged husky gets in on the action.

While they're stealing all the attention, Thom Yorkie, my five-pound, one-eyed killer, yaps at my office door.

My stomach clenches. I know who's on the other side.

My operations manager, Alan, waltzes into my office uninvited. "Calm down, dude, I'm just bringing your mom dinner." He holds up two bags.

"Taco Bueno," I cry. "I love you!"

Rapid blinking amazement appears on his face.

Great, now I'll never get rid of him. I stupidly used the L-word. Alan takes that word very seriously.

I roll over on all fours, forgetting about my injured limb. The pain hits my head first, and I almost pass out.

Alan drops the bags on my desk and rushes over. "Why aren't you wearing the sling?"

"I'm a graphic designer. Can't do my job with it on."

He moves behind me. "I'll give you a massage."

And there goes my appetite.

I never should have slept with him. A blizzard hit Denver over Thanksgiving weekend, and I was stuck at home with no license, after my DUI. Out of sheer loneliness, I ended up in bed with him. Afterward, he professed his undying love for me.

"From the moment I met you, I wanted you," he'd said, after giving me mediocre head.

It was all so horribly cliché.

After sleeping with him, a compilation of his endless good deeds over the years played through my mind. He takes care of my dogs when I'm out of town, which is huge considering Thom Yorkie bites him. Every. Single. Time.

There was the time he left his sister's wedding to change my flat tire.

Another time, he insisted on cleaning up the poo water in my bathroom after my septic tank backed up.

Who does that?

In case you were wondering, "a good friend" is the wrong answer.

As we speak, he's regarding me with the same intensity as my dogs—all of them desperate for my taco.

The morning after "the incident," I set him straight. "I don't do relationships." Not after dating that man whose name begins with E and ends in piece-of-shit.

God, I didn't even think of his full name, and I'm irate.

Anyway, after I told Alan the part about no relationships, it was like a nuclear bomb blew off his face. We're talking major devastation. So I softened the blow. "Let's not rush into anything."

"I'm not going anywhere," he told me.

I'm not going anywhere. Has a creepy ring to it, doesn't it?

Ever since "the incident," I've been avoiding him. I work all day with my door closed. If this keeps up, I'll have to work from a remote island.

And that's precisely what I plan to do when I win this pitch. I haven't taken a vacation in years. I'm tired of owning an agency. I'm tired of being a boss. I'm just tired.

I haven't told a soul, but once I win Proton Sports' new business, I'm getting out of here. Grayson Advertising wants to buy me out. The problem is Grayson needs to see a higher profit margin. They don't want to lay off staff or pay creditors during the acquisition.

This new business is my ticket out of here. It's the extra boost I need to sell this joint.

My godparents, Burt and Art, own Proton. We already handle their retail business. This adult camp is a side-venture of theirs. If it does well, they plan to expand. It's a huge opportunity, and also why I've been working so hard on the campaign.

I don't know why I'm bothering. We're a shoo-in to win this business. The Orion Agency caters to the sports and outdoor market. It's what differentiates us from Shimura, the rival agency. They won an award for an RV campaign a year or so ago, but they don't have anywhere near the amount of experience we do.

This pitch will be a piece of cake. And once we win, I'm out of here. Out of this office. Out of this state. Out of this country.

Out of this world. I want a clean slate and fresh memories. I want an adventure. I want to live again.

I want to get off my Prozac.

But no one else knows that.

"Miss Perky." That's what my receptionist, Christine, calls me. "I pray to Jesus every night that he'll make me as happy as you."

I'm pretty sure Jesus doesn't take personal requests. Otherwise, my family would still be alive.

My receptionist is a little obsessed with the Lord. But after running through secretaries like toilet paper at a beer festival, I'm totally cool with her saying "grace" at the vending machine.

Speaking of machines, Christine is one. Her athletic prowess is going to help me win this pitch.

Proton asked me to put together a team of eight "sporty" people for the pitch, and she's number one. Alan's number two.

I know what you're thinking, why invite a man who drives me insane to Breckenridge for two weeks? I'll tell you why: his parents ran a camp in the Catskills for ten years. I need his firsthand knowledge. He's a kick-ass skier, too. And he's also breathing down my neck. *Ick.*

I back my chair away from him.

He picks up a notepad on my desk and reads it out loud. "Joy, Duffy, Stanley, Wang, Christine...Is this the final team list?"

I snatch back my notepad. Just because he's been in my vagina doesn't mean he has the right to riffle through my things. "Yep."

"This ought to be interesting," he says.

Ain't that the truth.

Maybe I can manufacture a sudden case of herpes to get rid of him. Except that would be the immaculate infection, since I've never slept with anyone without condoms and a stiff birth control pill prescription.

"I better get the boys home," I tell him.

"Let me drive you. It's snowing."

A few months ago, I lost my license in a drunk-driving accident. It was stupid, and I'm lucky I didn't hurt anyone. I had a few happy hour drinks and slid on a patch of ice. Totaling my car was no fun. Neither was spending the night in jail.

Alan had to bail me out. Another reason why I'm indebted to him.

Good thing I only live three blocks away from the office, otherwise I'd have to take him up on the offer. "No, thanks," I say. "The boys and I prefer to walk." *And I can't stand your hands on me—they're like a swarm of mosquitos.* "Goodnight."

"Night," he mumbles and slump-walks away like Charlie Brown after getting a rock in his trick-or-treat bag.

Outside, I slosh through the dirty snow to my loft. Once there, I don't bother to turn on the lights. I just crawl into bed with the wet dogs and stare into blackness until I fade out.

THREE

Eli Goes Home

Eli's Mixtape: Mike Watt, "E-Ticket Ride"

OUTSIDE OF BRECKENRIDGE, COLORADO
We're in the van to Breckenridge and Skip tells the driver to stop in front of a marijuana dispensary. "Anyone need anything?"

Avery looks like she's ready to fight Skip to the death. "You are not stopping this van to buy drugs. Can't you see my child is upset?"

"You're kidding?" he says dryly. "That sweet angel who didn't stop screaming the whole flight is upset?"

She stabs a finger at him. "Not one word. Not one complaint from you. This is your fault."

"I'm not complaining. I'm medicating." Skip opens the door and gets out. "BRB."

I'm not a pot guy, but I sure could use a little natural anxiety medication right about now. Flying next to Sabrina was a real treat. After four hours of her begging to get back together, it feels like someone hacked open my skull with an ax.

Or it could be this place. My first glimpse of those snow-capped purple peaks brought back every single crushing moment of my tortured youth.

Home is where the broken heart is.

Forty years later, Skip jumps back in the van with a lawn and leaf bag-sized sack of weed.

Avery scoffs. "What is that? Like a grand worth of drugs?"

My boss narrows his eyes to black slashes. "Thou shalt not throw stones at grass houses, Miss 'Candy Hoarder' Adams."

She gasps. "Are you calling me fat?"

"No, I'm calling you judgy." Skip sits next to her kid and waves a brownie in front of his face. "Want some cake, little boy?"

Avery snatches the brownie. "Are you even human?"

"That's a real brownie, Adams, not an edible."

"The hell it is."

"I'm serious. Try it."

"Cake. Cake!" chants her kid.

"Avery, I swear it's not laced."

She unwraps the brownie, sniffs it, and takes a tiny bite. "Tell Skip thank you, Austin."

"Tank you, Austin!" says the kid. For a two year old, he's a pretty smart little dude.

We arrive at the place twenty minutes later.

"Holy moly, this isn't like the camp I went to," Jerry mutters as he yanks his four-ton suitcase out of the van. "I was expecting teepees."

The sprawling lodge is decked out with sparkling Christmas lights and big pine wreaths with bright red bows. It's three stories high and built like a log cabin. In the distance, there's a lake and a barn and a vast sea of white.

"Okay, smiles everyone, smiles," Skip says with zero excitement.

Sam bounces and rubs his arms. "It's cold as balls up here."

"This is nothing," I tell him. "When the sun goes down, it'll drop forty degrees."

His teeth chatter. "Hope they have dark liquor to warm me up."

We trudge up the icy walkway and ring the doorbell. A minute later, a stocky, leathery man with a gray buzz cut, a gray flannel shirt, gray jeans, and suspicious gray eyes opens the door. He's wearing pink bunny slippers. "I'm not interested in the teachings of Christ," he says in a Clint Eastwood-bad-guy-gruff and slams the door.

Skip backs out and looks at the address. "Did our driver ditch us at the wrong place?"

Avery's kid starts to cry.

The door swings open, and a hefty bald man steps out. "Burt's just messin' with you guys. Come on in and get warm by the fire. I'm Art, the co-owner of Proton." He shakes everyone's hands. "Just leave everything here in the lobby. Our camp counselor, Malcolm, will haul everything to your rooms, later."

"Oh, no, I won't," someone—presumably Malcolm—shouts from another room. "I jacked up my back hauling firewood."

All of us don big, client-facing faux grins. Nothing wrong here. This is all perfectly normal.

We follow the two men into a mammoth den. On the ceiling, the pink sunset shimmers through the skylights. A ginormous stone fireplace takes up an entire wall. Rustic leather couches and sheepskin chairs face a crackling fire. Above the mantel there's a pink stuffed buffalo head that looks like a Muppet.

Art catches me staring at it. "In the other room, we have a purple pleather rhinoceros head to go with it. My friend in Grand Junction makes them."

"Awesome," I lie. This is what you do in front of a potential client, lie and pretend you're having a great time with a pink buffalo head at an isolated winter camp with seven coworkers.

Art chuckles and steps in front of Avery. "Who do we have here? Is this Austin?" He tickles the little boy's quivering chin.

"You look like you could use some hot chocolate with marshmallows." He holds out his hand. "May I?"

Austin hides behind her legs.

"Oh, I don't know," she says. "He's had a lot of sugar. He's a little wild right now."

"Aw, all boys are wild," Art says in a baby voice.

"Bad man," Austin says.

"Take the kid to the kitchen, Adams," Skip tells her.

She smiles back a silent "fuck you" and coaxes her boy in that direction.

Burt swaggers over, looking like he's about to pistol-whip some sense into me. He grips my hand in a death squeeze and scrunches his face up like he's staring at the sun. He's six inches shorter, but seems ten feet taller.

"How was the flight?" he asks.

I yank my hand. He won't let go. "Fine. Good. Great."

"I wasn't asking you, Bearded Clam."

I dart my gaze around the room. "Did you just call me—?"

"Bearded Clam? You bet your ass I did. What's that fur on your face? Think you're one of them hipsters?"

First of all, I hate the word hip. Only people who aren't hip use that word. Second of all, it's not like I'm Gandalf. My beard is more like scruff. And if I didn't have it, I'd look like a teenager instead of a thirty-one-year-old man.

I pry his fatal grip off of me. "Great place you have here."

"Blah, blah, blah. Quit your yapping, girly man."

I glance at my coworkers. They look equally perplexed.

"Malcolm!" Burt shouts, still glaring at me.

A man with bright red hair limps out with a hand on his back. "Stop yelling, old man."

"Malcolm's the head counselor here."

"More like the head slave," he mumbles.

Burt squints at him. "Take these folks to their rooms so they can freshen up. We'll meet downstairs at seventeen hundred and go over everything when the other team gets here." He stabs a finger at me. "Maybe think about shaving that vagina off your face, Princess."

Did Skip dose me between here and the weed store? This can't be real.

Upstairs, Malcolm points down a hallway. "Pick any room you want. I'll let you fight over the ones with private decks and hot tubs." He holds out his hand for a tip.

Jerry slaps Malcolm's hand. "Thanks, man. Appreciate it."

The camp counselor regards Jerry as if he's the most rancid-smelling man alive.

I hand the guy a five, and he bows with no trouble then limps down the stairs holding his back.

Skip takes me aside. "St. James, what's up with *Pale Rider* downstairs? You know him from somewhere? Why's he giving you hell?"

"No idea, man."

"He does kind of look like *Dirty Harry*," Jerry says.

"Shut it, Jerry, no one asked you," Skip grumbles.

"Back in India," Preeti chimes in, "Dirty Harry's voice is dubbed with a high-pitched old man who sounds like he's missing a testicle." She cracks up.

Skip blank-faces her.

She shrugs.

Skip pinches his chin. "Dirty Harry's problemo with St. James presents a challenge. New plan: I want the ladies to charm the bunny slippers off that guy, and keep *Pale Rider's* mind off St. James. St. James, you stay away from him. Maybe shave off that beard."

"Screw that guy. I'm not shaving off my beard."

Skip strolls down the hall, dragging his luggage and bag of pot. "I'm betting door number eight has a hot tub with my name on it. See you kids in a bit, after I get nice and baked."

I choose door number one, which unfortunately does not have a hot tub. It does, however, have a private deck that faces the lake. I slide open the door and step outside.

Off in the distance, a woman with long brown hair and a red knit beanie slogs through knee-high snow with four dogs bouncing behind her. One dog only has three legs, but it doesn't slow him down. A tiny squirrel of a dog runs behind him, yapping like crazy.

I shiver. Something about her reminds me of Charlie and her crew of strays.

Colorado is full of ghosts, and they are going to haunt me this whole trip.

On the bed is Proton's survival guide. I crack open chapter one and read.

"Many survival sagas begin with lost campers."

Survival Tip*: Sometimes a collision occurs without warning, but in most instances, there is a premonition that something is about to happen.*

Eli's Mixtape: Twenty One Pilots, "Stressed Out"

AFTER A QUICK NAP, I amble downstairs to the den. The rest of my agency, minus one sleeping toddler, is spread out on the leather sectional on one side of the room. Our competition, the Orion Agency, is seated across from us.

They seem like the typical ad agency peeps: unapproachably smug and, dare I say, hip?

A studious-looking Asian guy with glasses is parked next to a Goth girl with gobs of eye makeup. Another dude with a long, gray ponytail is sitting cross-legged on the floor. Big surprise, he's wearing a Grateful Dead shirt.

A woman with corded muscles like a bodybuilder reclines

next to the Deadhead, fingering her cross and mumbling to herself. *One of these things is not like the others.*

One guy is staring out the window. Brown hair, brown eyes, khaki pants—he's got to be the accountant.

Another happy-go-lucky lanky man is standing by the fireplace. There's no way that guy works in creative. He's probably an account manager.

The guy at the window steps next to Proton's owners. "This place is incredible. When are you planning on opening it up to the public?"

"Sit down, Alan, you ass kisser," Burt says.

Apparently, I'm not the only one *Pale Rider* has a problem with. And the guy doesn't have a beard.

"Where's your fearless leader?" Art asks the other agency.

A herd of dogs bounds up on the deck outside.

Art turns to the sliding glass door. "Ah, there she is, with her hellhounds."

The woman from the lake backs in and stomps her feet on the mat. The dogs run past her and shake out their wet coats.

"Sorry, I'm late," she says. "My useless sled-dog refused to pee in the snow." She laughs at the absurdity.

The sound of her voice is like metal crunching in a car wreck.

That voice. It belongs to the same woman who sliced out my heart ten years ago.

A scarf covers her face, but I don't need to see it. It's her.

Charlie.

My body breaks out in a cold sweat as I watch her unravel her scarf like I'm watching a scene in a horror movie.

She removes her coat and hat and shakes out her long gingerbread mane. The same wispy flyaway strands float down her rosy cheeks. And her eyes are still the color of warm maple syrup.

The last time I saw her, they were vacant, almost black.

I'm paralyzed.

One of her dogs toddles over, wagging its tail, and buries its nose in my crotch.

I still can't move.

"Julius Seizure! Bad boy." She springs over with the same bouncy tomboy gate. "Sorry, he's got a thing for men's crotches —" Then her gaze smashes into mine.

Everything inside me dries out and twists into barbed wire.

She brings a trembling hand to her mouth. "Elliott."

Then she bolts off, leaving me fighting for air.

FOUR

Charlie Meets A Boy

August 1995

TODAY, Weiner brought home a boy named Elliott St. James. I like his blond hair and blue eyes. He looks like a Ken doll. Sir-Farts-A-Lot won't stop humping his leg. Dogs are an excellent judge of character.

February 1996

Elliott gave me a Valentine's Day card. It said 'Be Mine.' I told him I was already his.
    He turned as red as the heart on the card.

FIVE

Charlie Goes Bald

Eli's Mixtape: Blur, "Song 2"

IF THERE WERE an Olympic event in body hair removal, I would have just crushed the competition. I have never shaved so fast in my life, as evidenced by the seventy-three bloody toilet paper wads around the sink.

I didn't bring makeup. I didn't bring a hairbrush! I was trying to look as ugly as possibly so Alan would leave me alone.

All I packed were sports bras and ugly period panties. And sweatpants. I don't even wear sweatpants. I bought them at Wal-Mart just for this event. My clothes are old and comfy and totally ugly.

What was I thinking? I'm going to have to go shopping. Maybe Malcolm will sneak me out of here and drive me to Vail.

This is not happening. My ex-boyfriend is not downstairs.

His hair is just as thick and blond as it was in college. And he's just as fit and muscular as he was when he was training for the Olympics. He has a beard now, and more tattoos, but that's the only difference. If anything, he's more handsome.

How dare he look so good! Why couldn't he have gotten bald or fat?

Did he have a ring? What if he's married? *This is a nightmare.*

I've been telling myself he was dead. That was the only way I could accept it. *But, oh, no.* He's alive and downstairs, sipping sherry by the fire. Or drinking beer. Or whatever.

That bastard! When I get a hold of him, he's going to wish he were dead.

In the mirror, a beast of a woman finger combs her hair with wild jazz hands. This is a disaster. I'm a disaster. I'm hyperventilating.

I slump to the floor and put my head between my knees.

Listen up, Charlotte! You will not let that Nordic obstacle get in your way. You will win this competition, no matter what. You are successful. You are talented. And you are carefree and bubbly.

I get up and hide the bottle of Prozac in my nightstand.

And you will not look at him.

Don't look at him, I remind myself on the way to the living room. His crystal blue gaze is as dangerous as Medusa's.

I flash a thousand-watt fake smile around the room and plunk down next to Christine. "Sorry, I'm late. Thanks for waiting."

The head camp counselor, Malcolm, passes around a plate of chocolate chip cookies.

I take one and smash it into paste.

"Let's get started," Burt says. "First off, Camp Proton is a digital-free zone. Let your people know they can call the front desk if there's an emergency, because we're taking your devices."

A roar of displeasure erupts around the room.

Burt rubs fakes tears from his eyes. "What a bunch of wussies. Can't communicate without technology? Wah!"

"That guy's kind of a dick," Joy whispers. My art director's personality doesn't match her name. We call her *Eeyore* around the agency, because she's ever the complainer. That said, she's an amazing web designer.

"It's just an act," I tell her. That man is as soft as they come.

Art flips over a dry-erase board and taps it with his knuckles. "Breakfast, lunch, and dinner will be at these hours in the dining hall. Scoreboard's over in the corner. At the end of the retreat, the team with the most points wins the business."

Malcolm showcases the team names like Vanna White on *Wheel of Fortune*.

ORION AGENCY		SHIMURA AGENCY	
CHARLIE SULLIVAN Chief Creative Director		**SKIP SHIMURA** CEO	
ALAN FOSTER Chief Operating Officer		**ELI ST. JAMES** Senior Art Director	
CHENGLIE WANG Head of Search & Analytics		**AVERY ADAMS** Associate Creative Director	
JOY GORDON Senior Web Designer		**JERRY RENO** Finance Manager	
DUFFY LANGSTON Senior Copywriter		**SABRINA TATE** Account Manager	
CHRISTINE MOORE Receptionist		**SAM FISCHER** Senior Web Developer	
STANLEY WRIGHT Account Director		**PREETI DESHPANDE** Marketing Intern	

Wang raises his hand. "Are those Bitmojis?"

"You like?" Malcolm asks.

"No," Elliott says.

Personally, I love his avatar. Nothing's more fabulous than seeing your ex on a stripper pole with deely boppers. Serves him right.

On the other team, a stunning man, who must be Skip,

based on the avatar, wanders over to the chart. "Why are you keeping score? What about our campaigns?"

"Shimura, I don't care about your pretty pictures and headlines," Burt tells him.

So he *is* Skip Shimura. He doesn't look like he's from New York at all. He looks more like he belongs in Boulder with his black, floppy anime haircut.

Burt continues his rant. "Any old agency can come up with that crap. I want to know your personalities and how well you work together. I want to know your strengths and weaknesses and how innovative you can be in the face of a challenge."

"But you already know us," my account manager says. Stanley is a six-foot-seven sweetheart and a single dad. His daughter is deaf. He's the most patient man alive.

I love Stanley, but I think my account manager's pleasant personality grates on Burt's nerves.

"I don't know anything about you, flower petal. My marketing manager throws work in your lap, and you make pretty pictures. That's all I know."

Art takes a gentler approach. "Proton is already the number one sports retailer in the nation. The company runs itself. But this lodge is our retirement dream. It's where we want to grow old together."

Burt blushes and continues. "So now you know what's at stake."

A guy on the other team, who looks like he just stepped off the set of the *Sopranos*, speaks up. "Youse guys are gay?"

Burt puffs out his chest. "You got a problem with that?"

The guy salutes Burt. "No, sir. It's just you're really… *masculine*."

"Shut.Your.Mouth.Jerry." Shimura looks like he's going to take that meathead out.

"So what exactly are we doing here, Burt, if we're not presenting our campaign?" Alan asks.

An evil grin breaks out on Burt's face. "We're gonna have

you go through the program and play all the games, just like regular campers."

Elliott straightens. "What?"

"You heard me, Bearded Clam."

A nervous giggle bursts out of me. I flick a glance at Elliott. He's staring right at me.

My stomach flutters, and involuntarily, I smile.

He turns away.

I keep the smile pasted to my face.

"So tonight," Burt says, "we'll celebrate the opening ceremonies at dinner. Then at oh-eight-hundred tomorrow, we'll have us some fun." He winks at me, glances at Elliott, then back at me.

Burt doesn't know about my ex, otherwise I'd think he was up to something.

"Uh, like, when is oh-eight-hundred?" asks a supermodel on the other team. She's tall, blonde, perfect, and the polar opposite of me. And she works with Elliott. And she's practically sitting on his lap. They're together.

I grab my stomach. *Why is this happening to me?*

"What's up with all the hot people on that team?" Joy whispers. "Do they have to take head shots to work there? Look at that lumber-sexual blond guy on the end. He looks like he'd be a fantastic lay."

He is. A phenomenal lay. "Joy, pay attention, please."

"Oh, I am." She waves at Elliott.

He wipes a hand across his mouth like he's sandpapering a wood floor.

Christine leans in. "Jesus is watching you, Joy."

Joy grabs her tits and jiggles them at Christine. "Is he watching this?"

I slump down in my seat. *Calgon, take me away.* Or better yet, where's the hard liquor in this joint? I need a cocktail ASAP.

My brazen hussy of an employee saunters over to Elliott and

holds out a hand as if she was a queen and he should kiss it. "Joy. And you are?"

"Eli." His voice is steady, manly, cheerful, nauseating. And he goes by Eli now, apparently.

That bastard.

While everyone mingles, I stare down at the cookie paste I've made.

Skip roams over and holds out a hand.

I show him the chocolaty mess.

His brows arch, probably because it looks like I'm playing with dog shit.

He sits and sighs. "So what are the chances we'll actually steal this business from you?"

Honestly? They don't have a prayer. But if he packs up and leaves, I'll never see Elliott again. And I need to tell that prick a few things before he leaves. So I lie. "I'll let you in on a secret. Burt's marketing manager hasn't been super pleased with us lately. We're just as desperate to win this as you." Well, that part is true.

"This shit's stressing me out," he says, not sounding the slightest bit stressed.

I glance at Elliott. "Me, too."

SIX

Eli Meets A Little Brat

Patrick's basement, Age 11

I WAS in the middle of an epic game of Space Invaders with my new friend, Patrick, when his bratty little sister stomped down the stairs and ripped the controller out of my hands.

"My turn, Weiner," she said to her brother and reset the game.

"Get out of here, Squirt! Boys only. Sorry about my little sister." Patrick nudged her out of the way.

That was a big mistake.

She hauled back and whacked her brother on the side of the head. "Sexist pig."

"That's your sister?" I couldn't believe such a beautiful creature could be related to this guy. She was only a year younger than us, but seemed far older. For one thing, she was as tall as her brother. And the way she ordered him around wasn't like any little sister I'd ever met.

She whipped a look at me, daring me to challenge her. "Who's your new friend?"

"Elliott," I told her.

"That's a geeky name."

"What's your name?"

She stuck her nose in the air. "Charlie."

"Charlie's a boy's name."

She raised a fist. "Do I look like a boy?"

No, she didn't. In fact, she was the cutest girl ever. But my reputation was at stake with her brother, so I made her an offer. "How about we make a bet," I said. "You beat me, you stay."

Patrick high-fived me. "No way she'll beat you, man."

She spit on her hand and held it out to seal the deal.

I glanced down at it.

She grabbed my hand and slapped it against her spitty palm. "Fire it up, Weiner."

The plan was to let her win so she could stay, but that wasn't necessary—she kicked my ass. And when she did, she danced around the room, wiggling her tiny butt and calling me loser.

"Want to stay for dinner?" she asked me later. "We're having fried maggots."

"In that case, count me in."

After that, I let her beat me almost every afternoon, just so I could stare at her.

❄

Survival Tip: Bad weather, poor communication, an injury—unexpected events such as these, can end up a disaster. You must imagine the worst possible scenario on your journey, and prepare for it.

Eli's Mixtape: Lean Year, "Come and See"

FOR THE REST of the night, I play a cool, professional game. It's dumb jokes before dinner, polite small talk during, drinks and bullshitting later, friendly games of pool after that, and the whole time, I act like I'm not really stroking out.

I'm serious. The whole left side of my body is numb.

In fact, I'm hiding in the bathroom right now, trying to regain feeling by sitting on the toilet, scrolling through my Buddhist quote app before I have to give up my phone, searching for one that will apply to my situation. "Detachment means letting go, and non-attachment means simply letting be."

What the fuck?

What am I going to do without my Buddhism app? I'm not going to survive.

Wait, that's attachment.

My hand is shaking. I'm a little bitch. I'm a coward. I'm weak.

Charlie hasn't changed at all. She's still "the girl next door" meets "private school porn star."

Always the walking contradiction—aloof yet affectionate, strong and soft, raw and cultured, sweet and dangerous, wild as hell and calm as...

Never mind. She's not the slightest bit calm. In fact, she's insane. I'm not kidding. The rest of it though, I'm not making it up. She's a puzzle made up of a million pieces—impossible to figure out.

Okay, here's what I'm going to do. I'll go with the flow. For now, I'll be Mr. Serene. I am a chill motherfucker from here on out.

My ex is not here. I won't look at her. I won't speak to her.

If anything, that'll piss her off.

Serves her right.

When I vacate my hidey-hole, almost everyone has drifted off to bed. Including her.

Time to escape.

I slip on my boots and coat and head outside. Other than the snow crunching under my feet, the only sound is my racing thoughts.

The moon has vanished behind the mountain range, and the cold pinches my nostrils. The air is so thin and clean it hurts to inhale. Every step takes twice as much effort.

The smell out here—burning pine and metallic wind—it brings back awful memories. This is where life ends.

My collar feels like a noose. I tug at it the whole way back to the lodge.

Instead of using the front door, I hop over the lower deck. In the dark, a hot tub bubbles and steams. Someone must have forgotten to put the cover on.

I shed my clothes where I'm at and step into the tub. The brisk air and hot liquid prick my limbs as I settle into a corner seat in front of the jets.

I sink under the water and listen to the motor churn above me, searching for the chill motherfucker who has completely abandoned me in my hour of need.

When I come up for air, there's a naked woman on the other side with her eyes closed.

Charlie.

I study her like a painting at a museum. Her body is just as succulent as it was in college. Full breasts and long, lean legs. She's thinner now; her ribs are showing. Giant black and yellow bruises cover her shoulder and chest.

Who did that to her? Was it her boyfriend? Her husband? My mind goes crazy, and I rise up from the steam on fire.

An unholy scream rips out of her lungs. She splashes and slips, attempting to flee for her life.

"Shh! Charlie. It's me, Eli."

Bare ass facing me, she hugs herself and lowers back under the bubbles. "Jesus! Why didn't you say something?"

I don't have a reason I feel like admitting, so I don't give her one. "What happened?" I nod to her injury.

"I dislocated my shoulder hang gliding."

Her happy adventure injury upsets me even more. She's

been living the dream apparently—running her own business, hang gliding.

I reply with controlled ambivalence. "Pretty dangerous sport."

She skips over the subject and grabs her throat. "I almost had a heart attack when I saw you earlier. I think I'm still in shock." A weird laughter tumbles out of her. Nervous laughter. Fake laughter.

I push a hand through my wet hair. "Same here. Uh, I mean, the heart attack part. I see myself every day." *Ugh, what the hell am I saying?* I'm eleven years old again.

Another weird giggle froths up. Then silence stretches between us.

"It's good to see you again, Elliott. I guess you go by Eli now?"

"And you're not Charlie anymore." There's hostility in my tone. It's on purpose.

A glazed look floods her expression. "After the accident, I started using my full name."

The hot water is now a sea of ice. *The accident.* I was hoping I'd never hear that word again.

She sees something in my expression and changes the topic. "So what have you been up to for the last ten years? Thought you'd end up a being a rock star." She laughs again. "You and Patrick and your grunge band that you wouldn't let me join." She curls a fist and shakes it at me.

I allow myself a smile. "I'm still a musician." I leave out the part where I'm a retired club DJ. "What about you? Thought you were going to be a veterinarian?"

Her mouth sags. "I was, but my parents didn't leave a will, and I had to pay off their debt. I went to community college instead."

The wind blows snow off a nearby tree branch onto my head. I leave it melting on the back of my neck.

I want to ask her more, but I can't, because it hurts.

"Is it weird to be back in the motherland?" she asks.

"Yeah."

"Lots of memories, I'm sure."

I glance up at the black sky.

"Do you miss it here?"

The question has a deeper meaning. She wants to know if I've missed her. I meet her gaze. Charlie can say five things at once with one look. Right now she's telling me her life hasn't been that great. And it's my fault.

"No," I say and leave it at that.

Her hand flies to her shoulder like I've just shot a poison arrow in it, but her tone is still fruity and light. "Soo…are you and the pretty blonde dating? The one who can't take her eyes off of you?"

A bolt of anger zaps me. I surge up from the water, clutching my exposed balls, and try not to shout when the cold air smacks my nuts.

"Don't go," she pleads.

I jerk on my jeans over my wet body and zip up my jacket over my bare chest. Chilled all the way to my soul, I stand with my back facing her. "I can't do this, Charlie. I just…*can't*."

"Elliott." Her voice barely rises above the sound of the jets.

I bundle the rest of my clothes under my arm and race to the door. Just before I shut it behind me, I catch her mumbling.

"Fuck off then, you fucking hot son-of-a-bitch. Why don't you get some more hot tattoos and work out some more on your hot body, you hot fucking shitbag. Fucker. Fuck face. God, I'm such an idiot."

A wide grin engulfs my face. That's better. That's the Charlie I remember.

That night, I don't sleep. All I can think about is her—the last woman I want to think about.

SEVEN

Charlie Knows Sex

November 1997

Dear Diary: I know about sex. It's where two people get naked and kiss. Some people do it over and over again. You can get sick and die of AIDS. See ya later!

Later that week

I've been thinking Elliott and I should do "it." We've already kissed. He's the most beautiful man alive. He's so nice and wonderful. I love him. He loves me. We should just do it and get it over with. Then we can be boyfriend and girlfriend for reals.

I stole *The Joy of Sex* from my parents' room. The couple in the book is super ugly and has lots of hair. They look like Cro-Magnons. I wonder if Elliott has hair down there? I have three.

Later that same week

Mom found my diary and grounded me for a week. I've never

been so humiliated in all my life. She said I'm too young to have sex, and she called Elliott's mom and dad. He told me he didn't get in trouble. I asked him if he was mad at me, and all he did was smile.

EIGHT

Charlie Just Can't

Eli's Mixtape: Portugal. The Man, "Feel It Still"

ALL NIGHT, flashbacks shook me like bomb blasts. PTSD—triggered by him.

It's scary how much I blocked out from back then. But one thing I remember like it was yesterday: Elliott walking out on me.

It was a terrible time. And I made a terrible mistake. But I was blinded by grief. What was his excuse?

"I just can't, Charlie."

Can't what? Explain why he left me when my whole family died? Dick.

I thought he'd be there for me, no matter what. That was back when I believed in love. Mistakes aren't allowed in real relationships. Forgiveness is a figment of fairy tales.

In real life, it's either love or hate.

And right now, it's hate. Hate is the only thing fueling me. Otherwise, I'd stay in bed all day.

I'm the last one at the breakfast table. A buffet is set up in the corner, and I pile my plate with food I won't eat.

"How'd you sleep?" Alan asks.

The black circles under my eyes should be a dead giveaway. He's so clueless. "Great!" I say and find a seat away from him.

"I slept like crap," Joy says. "Wang's snores broke the sound barrier last night. It was like a herd of elephants trampling through my brain."

Wang's my Google guy. I imported him from China. He's a genius when it comes to search optimization. He and Joy are like brother and sister. They remind me a lot of Patrick and I.

Wang pushes his glasses up on his nose. "Was that before or after you watched porn on your iPad?"

"Shh!" Joy checks to see if Burt heard at the other end. "I am *not* giving up my iPad. There's too much incriminating evidence on that thing."

"I'll be knocking on your room tonight at twenty-hundred, then," he informs her.

Their banter is usually the highlight of my day. It's like a comedy routine. Today, I want them to shut up and stop having fun.

I sneak a peek at Elliott. He's chatting with Avery and her little boy. They're having a grand ole time, laughing and playing.

He catches me staring at him, and the cheer slides off his face like melted butter.

Hear that? It's the echo of his screams when I shank him later.

I wave my team in. "Let me make it clear to you all right now—nothing, I repeat, *nothing* is more important than winning this business. I want heads in the game, people. This is no joke." I bang my knife on my plate for emphasis.

My receptionist, Christine, makes a horrible suggestion. "How about we all take hands and pray?"

I tap the knife against my temple. "How about we get our heads in the game instead."

Before she has a chance to guilt-trip me, Art stands at the

head of the table. His bald head is polished to a shine. "All right, gang, while you're finishing up, I'll go over the rules for today's broomball game."

"Yes!" Jerry, the steroidal dude on the other team, tries to fist bump Skip.

Skip volleys back a blank stare.

Art lists a bunch of mumbo jumbo. When he's done droning on, Malcolm drags in a huge pile of rubber and drops it on the floor.

Burt blows an ear-shattering whistle. "Get suited up and head down to the lake."

"What are those?" I ask Wang.

"They want us to wear sumo wrestler costumes." He gives me a pleading look. "Please don't make me do this."

"What? No way!" I march over to Burt. "I'm not wearing that."

"You forfeit the business, then?"

"This is unprofessional," I snarl.

"So what?" he says.

Art rests a hand on Burt's shoulder, cutting off his abrasiveness. "Charlotte, loosen up for once. It'll be fun."

The meathead cackles. "That's what she said."

Skip slices a hand through the air like a cleaver. "Shut it, Jerry."

Art continues. "Once you're pumped up, head on down to the lake, and we'll get started."

"That's what sh—"

Sam, Shimura's edgy developer, shoves Jerry. "Stop talking."

That Jerry dude's chest may look like a Thanksgiving turkey, but I wouldn't want to mess with Sam. That guy looks like he knows about a hundred and fifty ways to assassinate.

Twenty-minutes later, sixteen fools, plus one toddler, roll down the hill in fat suits.

Joy falls flat on her face and struggles to get up.

I try to help her up and fall too.

Avery slips and slides into our pile.

I laugh so hard it comes out as silent gasps.

"Austin, help mama up." Avery reaches for her boy.

He jumps on top of her like she's a human bouncy house. It dislodges her from our pile and she zooms down to the lake with her boy on her bloated stomach, like she's a flesh-colored *Frosty the Snowman.*

Joy wipes away happy tears. "I haven't laughed this much since that time in college when I ate mushrooms and hung out with an Elvis impersonator."

I don't ask her to elaborate. That's just asking for trouble. "It's been a while for me, too."

Eli waddles by, then stops and lifts a corner of his mouth. A falcon flies overhead and screeches at the exact same moment. The deadly St. James smirk—breaking hearts for decades.

"Need help?" he asks.

"No!" I shout.

Joy holds out her mittened hand.

He takes it and jerks her to standing.

She flutters her eyelashes. "My hero!"

He politely offers a hand to me.

I blast him with a look so bloodthirsty it hurts my face.

The sexy smirk vanishes, as does he.

Joy watches him amble down the hill. "How does he manage to swagger in that sumo suit?"

"He's the enemy, Joy. Head in the game."

She pokes her tongue in her cheek. "Are you **PMS-ing?**"

I grit my teeth and toddle down to the ice, where the rest of my team awaits my orders.

My instructions are as follows: kill!

NINE

Eli is Once Bitten, Twice Shy

Survival Tip: *If you are bitten at any time, even if the bite heals and the wound seems benign, you MUST have it checked.*

Eli's Mixtape: The Kinks, "You Really Got Me (Remastered)"

IN THE SHELTER on the side of the lake, Skip calls us in for a huddle. "I have no clue how to play hockey, but I'm half Japanese, so I'm going to sumo the shit out of everyone while the rest of you win the game. Don't pass the ball to me."

Jerry proceeds to enlighten Skip about the rules of the game.

"Shut it, Jerry," he says, then pulls out his vape and takes a couple of tokes.

"Are you getting high in front of my child?" Avery whispers through her teeth.

Skip looks down at the kid and waves.

A whistle blows, and we put on our helmets and teeter out onto the ice with our brooms.

I scan the other team in search of Charlie. *Oh, there she is,* staring right at me. My stomach flips. For the rest of the game, she's invisible.

During the face-off, Jerry tells Stanley he's a pansy and then smacks the ball down the ice.

Sam runs after it and passes it to me.

I steady it with the broom and waddle down to the other team's net. Right as I'm about to smack it in, someone jumps on my back and topples me.

I roll over and see Charlie staring down at me with a wicked grin. "Loser," she mumbles and lumbers off.

It takes me a while to stand in the fat suit.

Meanwhile, Jerry steals the ball from the other team and scores.

Skip high-fives our finance guy. "Fuck yeah, Reno. Good work."

Skip's use of his last name makes Jerry work twice as hard on the ice, and he scores another right after that.

Later, Skip shoulders Wang, Orion's SEO guy, to the ground.

Wang makes the time out sign. "Penalty!"

Burt shouts back, "There are no rules in this game, boy. Get up and play."

A shoving match follows—Jerry against Duffy, the Deadhead on the other team.

While they're shouting obscenities at each other, Sam steals the ball and passes it to Avery.

She kicks it to Sabrina, who delivers it to me.

Once again, I line up the shot. Out of nowhere, Charlie rams into me and sends my broom flying across the lake.

She clutches her huge sumo belly and cackles. Abruptly, she stops and sneers. "You suck."

I meet her glare head on. "You're messing with the wrong fat man, sister. Don't turn your back."

"Ha!" She wobbles away with her gloved middle finger high above her head.

The whistle blows, and we're at it again. Five more times, Charlie body-checks me.

Every time she knocks me on my ass, Burt and Art laugh hysterically. "Ooof! That had to hurt! Hahaha! Get up, Beaver Beard, you big wussie. Hahaha!"

That's it!

Next time, I'm ready for her. Just as she's about to lunge, I step out of the way.

She crashes onto her shoulder and hisses.

The whistle blows.

I flop beside her. "Are you okay?"

Her teammate, Alan, rushes over and pushes me. "Are you hurt, honey?"

An angry red fog blows into my mind. Typical Charlie. She's with that clown, and yet she's hell-bent on making an ass of out of me.

"Charlotte and Bearded Clam!" Burt bellows. "You're out of the game."

"What!" I shout. "You said there weren't any rules."

Burt points to the lodge. "Out. Both of you."

I rip off my helmet and consider throwing it down on the ice. But that would make me look like even more of a doofus.

Charlotte flaps to her feet and waddles up the hill, gripping her shoulder.

I stomp after her, trip, roll down the hill, and get back up.

Burt and Art crack up again. "Watch yourself, Beaver Beard. Hahaha!"

I tear off the fat suit and leave it in the snow.

Back at the lodge, Charlotte can't lift her shoulder to take off the costume.

I reach for the Velcro fasteners on her back.

She smacks my hand away. "Don't touch me."

"I didn't mean to hurt you."

"Wouldn't be the first time."

Her dark daggers slice into me. I step back. "What's that supposed to mean?"

"I'm used to being hurt by you."

I scoff. "Oh, really? Is that what you told your boyfriend out there? That I'm the one who hurt you?"

She inches closer and rams a finger into my chest. "He's not my boyfriend, you…butthole!"

"What are we, in junior high again?"

"You son of a—!" She barrels into me, knocking me back on my ass. Then she piles on top of me and tries to punch my face.

I belly laugh. "You're like a Tyrannosaurus Rex. You can't hit me wearing that thing."

She bounces on top of me, trying to smother me with her sumo suit.

"You're gonna hurt yourself."

Tears sprout from the corners of her eyes. "I hate you."

"Hey." I brush a tear off her cheek.

She leans into my palm and closes her eyes. Her hair dangles in my face. It smells just like I remember—like strawberry bubble bath.

It comes rushing back—that horrible pang—the Charlie addiction. "Get off me."

She sniffles. "Not until you talk to me."

I flip her over and pin her arms.

Underneath me, she thrashes like a wild animal.

"Settle down, woman."

"Ow! My shoulder."

I release her hands.

Bad move.

She grabs my hair and rips.

"Ow! Shit!" I pin her hands back down and grin. "Aw. You're so cute when you're mad."

Her body stills, and her warm, syrupy gaze melts into mine. She licks her lips and closes her eyes. "I hate you."

My mind goes blank, and I bend over and bite her bottom lip.

She bites mine back.

We tear into each other like wild animals. The taste of her sweet breath, the silkiness of her lips, our gnashing teeth and hungry moans—it turns me into a savage.

Somehow, I get a hold of myself and let go of her arms.

Another bad move.

Once again, she grabs me, this time by the beard, and yanks.

I bite her neck hard and suck the bruised skin.

Then we're at it again, slamming our mouths together.

Outside, the sound of laughter drifts toward the lodge. I hop up and wipe my mouth.

She pushes herself up, wincing in pain.

My anger dissipates. "Let me help you."

"Leave me alone. Do what you did ten years ago, and just leave me the hell alone."

I fist my hair and shout at the ceiling. "What did you expect? You broke my fucking heart!"

"You broke mine!"

"You cheated on me!"

"You left me!"

My pulse bangs in my temples. "I didn't leave you. I took some time off to think!"

"You didn't tell me when you'd be back!"

"Five days! I was gone for five days, and you fucked someone else."

She turns away and whispers, "You left me."

At the worst possible moment, everyone bursts through the door. Orion's team is carrying a fake Stanley cup full of beer.

"We won!" yells the bodybuilder chick from the other team. "Joy scored the winning goal!"

Charlie's scowl snaps into a rubber band smile. "Awesome!"

Alan runs to her side. "How's your shoulder?"

That's my cue to leave. I stomp upstairs to my room and collapse on my bed.

Snow-plumped clouds gather in the skylight overhead.

I close my eyes and let the memory of our vicious kiss back in. A buried laugh escapes from my lungs.

Holy shit! What just happened? And how soon can I make that happen again? And how the hell can I get out of Colorado before it happens again?

When the madness wears off, the pain creeps in.

I did leave her. Because I couldn't face her. It took five days just to get up the courage to tell her I'd killed her whole family.

But I never got the chance, because she'd already moved on.

TEN

Charlie Goes To The Prom

Eli's Mixtape: Modern English, "I Melt With You"

May 2002

IT DIDN'T SINK in that my high school boyfriend had dumped me until he didn't show up to take me to the prom.

He and I had an argument over a blow job. I refused to give him one.

And there I was, all dressed up, waiting for him at the door, wearing makeup and heels.

I looked like an idiot.

Patrick and Elliott were home on break from their freshman year of college and witnessed the whole embarrassing thing.

I stared down at my bright pink fingernails and laughed it off. "Guess I better change."

"I'll take you," Elliott had said. "Give me thirty minutes to get ready."

I argued with him for ten of those minutes. Imagine the boy you've been crushing on for years asks you to the prom, but does it out of pity. I wasn't having it.

"Chicken," he said. "Just let me go get a goddamned suit."

My brother slapped his best friend's back on the way out. "I owe you. I was about to take her myself. And that's sick as hell, taking your sister to the prom."

True to his word, Elliott came back thirty minutes later, wearing a black suit, with a black shirt and a black tie and black Vans. He even bought me a corsage—a yellow orchid.

I hugged him so tight I smashed the flower all over his suit. I still remember the way he smelled—like snow and pine and crushed orchids.

He pinned it to my strap and rushed me out the door. "Let's go dance our asses off."

You know that part in the movie, *Grease*? Where everyone on the dance floor opens up to let Sandy and Danny on? It happened just like that.

Okay, I'm lying. No one gave a shit about us, but for me it was like a movie.

The disco lights flashed stars on Elliott's face and every song seemed like it was chosen just for us.

I was wearing this ridiculous pink dress, and my hair was as big as Pike's Peak, but I'd never felt so lovely, so womanly, so sexy.

Elliott always made me feel that way. I'm five-ten and not the slightest bit girly. But tucked under his tall frame, I felt as delicate and graceful as that orchid.

He gets me, I remember thinking at the time. *He understands me.*

That's what love's really about. We're all flawed. We're all messy. We all have baggage. But when someone dives in and happily swims around in your sea of weird, and you want nothing more than to float around in that person's pool of imperfections—that's love. And that's how I felt about him.

We danced and laughed until my giant hair fell into limp waves. And when the song "I Melt With You" came on—the world really stopped, and I melted against him.

We danced in a slow circle to that fast song, his hand curled around the nape of my neck, and as shockwaves ran down my core, I fretted for the end of the night when Elliott would turn back into my brother's best friend.

"Let's get out of here," he said.

And we ran.

He drove us in his beat-up Jeep to Red Rocks and parked along the road. He took off his jacket and handed it to me.

"It's closed," I told him.

"We're going up the side."

"I'm in heels."

"I'll give you a piggy-back ride." He opened my door and backed in. "Get on, Chicken."

I wrapped my arms and legs around him, and he lifted me up like I was light as a feather. He carried me to an outcropping on the side of the amphitheater then shimmied up the rocks and held out his hand.

I scampered up the smooth face, and we climbed to the top and sat down.

Below us, Denver's lights twinkled. And just over the horizon, Orion glowed brightly. "That's my favorite constellation," I told him.

He caressed my cheek. "You're my favorite constellation."

I turned to him, my mouth probably gaping open.

He lowered his lips just above mine. "Can I kiss you?"

I love that he asked. But it was completely unnecessary. I grabbed his tie and yanked him closer. "Yes. Oh, God, yes. Please, kiss me." Then I rammed my tongue down his throat.

He pulled away for a moment and laughed, then took my face in his hands.

"Oh, God," I said. "You're a face cupper."

"A face cupper?"

"Never mind. Shut up and kiss me."

I still remember the feel of his lips against mine, and the way his tongue dipped inside my mouth, ever so gently.

We made out until the birds started chirping and the sky

turned pink, and until our lips were bruised and my face was raw.

"I better get you home," he murmured against my neck. "Your brother's going to kick my ass."

On the way home, we held hands, and I thought, *this is it. He's finally my boyfriend.*

The minute we arrived, my brother stomped down the sidewalk and lit into Elliott. "Where the hell have you been?"

"Calm down, dude," Elliott told him.

"What did you do to my sister?"

I shoved my brother. "He took me to the prom. Now get out of my way."

Elliott bowed to me and gave me a shy smile. "Goodnight, Chicken."

Tears gathered at the base of my throat, but I smiled back and waved. "I had an amazing time."

"Amazing time, doing what?" Patrick shouted. "And why is your face all red?"

Elliott sighed and walked away, looking defeated.

I didn't see or hear from him again until I started college that fall.

My brother was the reason he never called, but it still broke my heart.

That didn't stop me from going to the same college as them. My plan was to get him back.

ELEVEN

Charlie Plays Party Games

Elliott didn't show up for dinner. He's gone. I just know it.

I stroke the bite on my neck and make inarticulate conversation. Everything hurts, worse than it did before.

When the dishes are cleared and Art instructs us to have a seat in the den, he finally arrives.

I want to leap out of my seat and run to him. Instead, I glower and mope. I'm a teenaged girl again.

Burt kicks back his recliner and folds his hands across his belly. "Well, well, nice of you to show up, Bearded Clam."

"Sorry, I fell asleep." There are pillow marks on the side of his face.

The urge to smooth the creases overwhelms me.

"Dinner's over, Sleeping Beauty," Burt tells him. "You snooze you lose."

Elliott grips the armrest and nods to my godfather. Most men would've said something rude. Not him.

Malcolm removes the corks from several bottles of wine and passes out glasses.

Alan sits far too close to me. My muscles twitch like a cat's back, repelling his touch.

"Hey," my COO whispers. "This is the first chance I've had to talk to you all day. Did you miss me?"

I demolish my glass of wine in one gulp then push out a weak smile. "Sure."

Art taps his glass with a corkscrew, and the conversation dies. "Back when I was a boy at camp, we played icebreaker games to get to know each other. Thought it'd be fun if we did the same. Malcolm will hand out the questions. Read them out loud, and then give us your answers."

Malcolm sighs dramatically then tosses folded-up pieces of paper in everyone's lap, muttering, "I never get a break around here."

I read my paper and slump down in my seat. "Oh, gawd."

Wang unfolds his and echoes my sentiment. "This blows."

Around the room, questions are silently read, and drinks are subsequently slammed.

Art beams a wide, devious grin. "Who wants to go first?"

No one raises a hand.

"All right, I'll choose." He points to Alan.

Alan reads his question. "If you could read anyone's mind in the room, whose would it be?" He smiles right at me. "Charlotte's. Although, I pretty much know what she's thinking all the time."

I raise my glass and snap my fingers. "Malcolm? More wine?"

He gives me an are-you-serious look. "Get it yourself."

While I'm topping off my glass, I consider pulling a French exit. That would look bad. Do I care?

"Skip, you're up next," Art says.

As quiet as a mouse, Skip reads his question.

"What's that?" Avery cups her ear. "Can't hear you?"

His eyes narrow to slits. "I *said*...name an achievement you're proud of." He mumbles something.

Avery shouts like an old woman with hearing problems. "Speak up!"

He pinches his forefinger and thumb across both eyelids. "Nothing," he grumbles. "I've done nothing with my life."

Avery loses the self-satisfied smirk and turns her attention to the fire. The room is dead quiet.

Art nods at me. "Charlotte?"

I take forever to unfold my question. "If you could revisit one day from your past, which would it be?" I swallow and stare directly at Elliott. "Senior prom."

Take that, you jerk. The best night of my life was with you. And for that matter, the worst night of my life was with you, too.

A shadow falls over him. He closes his eyes for a second then slowly opens them and stares out the window.

Charlotte scores a point for the team!

Christine goes on and on about how she was prom queen and won't shut up.

Art interrupts her and motions to Sabrina.

She reads her question. "Like, if you could see anyone in the room naked, who would it be?" Unlike me, she doesn't hesitate. "Eli."

The man of the hour closes his eyes again.

What is he doing? Meditating? Jerk.

"Haven't you already seen St. James naked?" Avery asks.

So it is true. They are together. I'm going to vomit.

"How about you go next, sunshine," Art says to Avery.

"Pass," she says.

"Read the question, Adams, or you're fired." Skip means it, too.

She reads it. "What's the one thing you regret most?" She picks lint off her sweater. "I regret that Austin doesn't have a dad. A real dad."

I'm not sure what her history is, but her answer seems to stun her coworkers into silence again.

Eli ruffles her hair. "Dads aren't everything, Ave. Mine was a joke."

Now it's my turn to be stunned. There's nothing wrong with

Mr. St. James. He was a loving father, albeit a kinky one. At least he *has* a father.

The wine burns a hole through my stomach. How much longer must this go on?

"Who's next?" Art says. "Jerry?"

Jerry stands and spreads out like the meathead he is. "If you were in a plane crash with everyone in the room, who would you eat to survive?" He doesn't even pause. "Easy. Avery."

Avery gasps. "What did you say?"

He shrugs. "You're the beefiest."

"You asshole."

I clasp my hands and beg. "Please, Art. Let's move on to something else."

He cuts me off. "Nonsense, I'm having a blast. Duffy, you're next."

My copywriter stands and recites his question. "If you could take back one thing you've said, what would it be?" He chuckles. "Told a fine lady at the grocery store the other day I was married. Been regretting that ever since."

No one laughs. Know why? Because this sucks.

"You're next, Wonder Kid," Art says to Wang.

"Describe your best quality." Wang attempts to look sexy. "My bedroom skills."

"Ha!" Joy shouts.

Are they sleeping together? How dare they! They better keep that on the down-low. If they cost me the merger, I'm going to…my mind goes blank. I'm too buzzed to come up with a threat. This strikes me as hilarious, and I blow out a severe case of snickers.

I'm spilling wine all over myself and all over the couch, and I can't stop.

Alan slides his hand over to my thigh. "What's so funny?"

My laughter fades, and I pick his mitts off of me. "I don't know." There is nothing funny about this moment.

Later, I find myself staring at Eli's knee—the one he busted in the snowboard accident. The doctor was right; he doesn't even have a limp.

I tip up my gaze. He's watching me. I smile and instantly regret it. I'm a nervous smiler. I smiled when the cops arrested me for that DUI.

He doesn't smile back.

Jerk.

Sam is called on. He reads his question. "Have you ever committed a crime? Yep," he says matter-of-factly. "Several. Daily."

Skip uncrosses his leg and sits up. "Are you serious?"

Sam shrugs. "Just being real."

"What sort of crime?" Joy sounds fantastically intrigued.

"Now that, you'll have to pry out of me." Sam winks.

"How about later tonight?" she says.

I can't take this anymore. "Are we done, yet? Good." I whistle to my dogs, slam my feet in my boots, and blast out the door.

It's snowing, just barely. Flakes land on my eyelashes, and I tilt my head back and open my mouth, letting them land on my tongue. Instead of feeling childlike, I feel old and ragged.

If only there were a time machine in which I could zoom back to the past and fix everything. I sigh. It probably wouldn't matter.

The dogs do their business, and I watch the party through the window. I can't go back in there. It's torture.

The hot tub on the lower deck is lit up. I let the dogs in, push off the heavy cover, and do a quick check over my shoulder before peeling off my clothes and stepping in.

Thom Yorkie yaps at the door. A shape looms behind him, and Eli steps out.

"Oh, no." I wave a finger. "Go back inside. There's only room for one in this hot tub."

"There's room for twenty in that thing." He steps closer. "How's your shoulder?"

I want to say, "What do you care?" but even as tipsy as I am, I can't be that immature.

Plus, my heart is pounding, and I secretly want him in the water with me.

In one move, he yanks off his sweater then pushes down his pants and boxer briefs. Steam pours off his ripped body. He stands naked in the arctic temperatures as if it's a balmy eighty-degrees.

He has no idea how to be insecure.

Gaze fused to mine, he steps in and lowers under the water.

It surprises me that he still has my feather tattoos on one bicep. I thought for sure he'd cover that up. On the other arm, he has a sleeve with a lotus flower in the center. It's as beautiful as his carved physique.

I can't stand it in here. It's like he turned up the heat to scalding hot.

We stare at each other, not saying a word. There's a power play happening. The tension is crackling.

"Are you doing this on purpose?" I ask.

"What?"

"Making me miserable?"

"That wasn't the plan." He drapes his arms across the back of the tub. "But if you insist."

Ferocity swells inside me. I want to slap that smirk off his face. "Why?"

"Why, what?"

His cockiness astounds me. "I see you grew up to be a complete asshole."

"Least I'm not a cheater."

I splash around in the water like a salmon swimming upstream, slipping and sliding to get at him. I raise my hand to slap him, and he grabs it and pins it behind my back, then hauls me into his lap.

"Calm down, Chicken. You're going to hurt your shoulder." He sounds amused.

It enrages me even more. "Let me go of me!"

He yanks my ponytail and bites my neck.

It hurts so good.

I execute a death squeeze with my thighs.

He bites my nipple then licks it.

It's ecstasy.

I shove my tit into his mouth, and he sucks it to the back of his throat.

I pinch his nipples.

He pinches mine.

I bite his neck.

His hand slides under the water and twists my clit.

I grab his cock in a stranglehold.

A feral growl breaks free, and his mouth crashes down on mine.

We are alpha wolves in the wild, trying to destroy each other.

He tugs me up and pushes me down over the side so my ass is in the air. "Didn't hurt your shoulder, did I?"

I don't feel anything but a raw throb between my legs. "No."

"Good." He cracks my ass so hard the dogs freak out at the door.

I reach around and grab his cock and give him a brutal hand job.

It's a blizzard, all of a sudden, and I can barely see. My exposed skin aches from the cold, but the parts under the water are sizzling.

He cups my mound and orders me to spread my legs.

My center liquefies. As does my brain. Without protest, I spread and back my ass against him.

His finger slides inside me.

I clench around it. "Fuck me."

"You want this? My hard cock in your wet cunt?" He taps his dick against me, and then twists another finger inside me.

"Your pussy's throbbing. I used to make you come so hard." His hand covers mine and jerks his dick faster.

"Make me come." I arch my back. "Fuck me."

And he does, with his fingers.

I glance over my shoulder. His hard-edged gaze doesn't belong to the man who used to adore me.

I pull away from him and scramble out of the tub. "I can't do this." My tone is bitter and sharp, just like his was last night. "You left me."

Scorn seizes his body. His muscles tense and ripple in the cold. Snow rages between us.

"Is that what you've been telling yourself?" The bite in his voice puts me on offense.

Frozen to the core, I square my shoulders and hold my head high, as if nothing bothers me.

"Pretty ballsy to revise the story when the character's right in front of you," he says.

I step back into the tub. "Isn't that what you're doing right now? Making up shit? Lying? Pretending you didn't fuck me over?" I shake my head. "I can't believe I ever loved you."

Agony replaces that angry spark in his eyes.

I win.

So why does it feel like I lost?

In an amazing display of false confidence, I take my sweet time getting out of the tub. It's bitterly cold, and I ache, but I parade toward the door like a queen and let myself in.

For a few seconds, I stand naked in the dark, shivering. Then I grab a towel off a shelf and sprint up to my bedroom, where I spend the night nursing the scars he slashed back open.

I hate him.

TWELVE

Eli Saves Dead People

Survival Tip*: Often during expeditions, people from different cultures and backgrounds are thrown together and forced into situations that call for considerable tact. SURVIVAL, however, must take precedence.*

Eli's Mixtape: Two Feet, "Love Is A Bitch"

I SIT cross-legged on the floor for hours, watching my reflection in the glass door as the sun rises like a ball of fire.

My intention was to meditate. It's obviously not working.

Then again, my intention last night was to clear the air, not fingerbang Charlie in the hot tub during a blizzard.

So much for my chill motherfuckerliness.

For years, I've been fantasizing about what I'd do if I ever saw her again. And that was not it.

I always pictured her blank-faced and unfeeling—like a robot.

The suffering mixed in with the snow on her lovely face—I

never imagined that. I never imagined she'd blame me as much as I've been blaming myself.

There is nothing worse than unintentionally hurting someone you love. Scratch that. There is nothing worse than killing someone's family.

In a really fucked-up way, I'm glad she cheated on me. It evens the score.

But I still can't get over it.

How dare she choose the prom as the best night of her life! That was *my* best night. She can't steal that from me.

At oh-eight-hundred I give up on my quest for peace, and go downstairs for breakfast.

Big shock—Burt gives me an earful. "Morning, Bearded Clam. Get enough beauty sleep?"

I briefly consider pounding in his face, but the ramifications would be too severe.

I'm relapsing.

"You will not be punished for your anger, you will be punished by your anger," Buddha said.

That's the last quote-of-the-day I received. I miss that app.

To go along with Burt's serving of insults, Charlie piles on a side helping of bitch face. She's out for my blood.

And it's adorable.

Her pale pink lips purse while her gaze pinches into a ridiculous excuse for a glare. Does she actually think she looks threatening?

I can't help but smile.

One evil eye still stuck to me, she reaches for a biscuit, and then brings it to her nose and smells it before she takes a bite.

I used to tease her about smelling everything. I snort when she smells her water.

She lobs another seething glare my way.

Suddenly, I'm hungry as hell for a challenge. I gulp down everything on my plate, fueling my body for a fight, feeling more alive than I have in years.

Burt blabs out the day's events. "Today's activities will take place at Breckenridge ski area." He takes a loud sip of coffee out of a mug inscribed with the words *Time to suck today's dick*, then continues. "The first team to the bottom wins. We'll meet up in the bar." And that's it. He dismisses us.

Sabrina raises her hand, and I brace myself for the stupidity about to follow.

"Like, I don't know how to ski," she says.

"Me, neither," Avery adds, bouncing her kid on her knee.

"Didn't say you had to ski down."

Sabrina raises her hand again. "Like, I don't know how to snowboard either."

Burt sets down his coffee and cracks his knuckles. "Be creative, people. That's what you do for a living, isn't it? Innovate? Can't ski or board? Figure out a way to get down the mountain without 'em." He looks at his watch. "We're loading up the van at oh-nine-hundred."

Sabrina raises her hand again.

Burt jams his hands on his hips. "What is it, professor?"

"Account manager, not professor. When is oh-nine-hundred?"

"For Christ's sake," Charlie grumbles.

The sting of embarrassment creeps up my face. My ex has figured out my other ex is a moron.

Art holds out his arms to Avery's kid. "How 'bout you and me go tubing, buddy?"

Austin replies with a scream. "Bad man!"

"You know two-year-olds are possessed by the devil, right?" Avery tells him.

"I fought in Vietnam," Art replies. "Think I can handle a toddler."

"Ha!" Avery says. "You have no idea…"

Skip blows out an exasperated sigh and pushes back his chair. "Adams, give the man the kid, and stop pretending the boy is a monster." He gestures us to follow him. "Quick team meeting in the game room before we head out."

When we arrive, Skip closes the door and pulls the laser pen from his back pocket. He shines it on all of us. "Who else knows how to get down the mountain, besides St. James and me?"

Sam raises his hand.

"You ski?"

He nods.

"How good are you?"

He smirks. "I'm all right."

"That's totally reassuring," Skip says flatly.

Jerry interrupts. "I'm just okay, too, boss. Ski a couple of times a year in Vermont. But it ain't nothing like these hills."

I'm expecting the usual "Shut it, Jerry," but this time Skip scrubs a hand down his face and mumbles, "We're doomed."

I chime in. "*Fistful of Dollars* out there said we just had to get down the mountain."

He perks up. "That's right, he did. Okay, team, let's think outside the box."

"Dude." I shake my head. "You did not just say 'think outside the box.'"

Skip blinks a hard stare at me. "Is this funny to you, St. James? You weren't giggling when She-Ra knocked you on your ass, yesterday. By the way, how does it feel to have your ass beaten by a woman?"

I'm no longer amused.

"Really, Skip?" Avery says. "You're pulling out the sex card?"

"I'll pull out Lil' Skipper and wield him like a weapon, if you don't shut up and figure out how to get your ass down the slope." He turns to the intern. "Ignore that remark."

Preeti looks horrified. "How can I?"

"So what's up with 'dat chick, anyway?" Jerry asks me. "You screw her mom or sumptin'? Why does she keep giving you dirty looks?"

"Shut it, Jerry," my boss and I say at the same time.

Skip burns our retinas with the laser one more time. "Ideas, people, I want them now."

"We could ski down," Sabrina says.

Skip air-strangles her.

"What about a sled?" Avery says.

"Not bad. Where would we get said sled?"

Sam leans against the pool table. "What about the snow patrol?"

Skip shines a red dot on Sam's forehead. "Fischer, I'm suddenly digging your criminal mind. Go on. How do we get the snow patrol's sled?"

Sam shrugs. "Break a bone? Head injury?"

"I like it," Skip says. "We have any fake blood laying around?"

Preeti speaks next. "How will you contact the patrol with no phone?"

Skip dislodges an iPhone from his hoodie pocket and waves it.

"How did you get that?" I ask.

He ignores me and carries on. "Who's pretending they're hurt?"

Jerry raises an enthusiastic hand. "I was an actor."

Avery turns to him with her mouth open. "You were?"

"Starred in an off-Broadway production of Annie."

"Stop right there," I say. "You played a white girl with a red afro?"

Skip cuts me off. "Make it look good, Reno."

Jerry's posture straightens at his boss's use of his last name. "Aye, Aye, Skipper."

Skip's upper lip climbs to an all-time high.

"Oh, I know!" Sabrina says. "What if we flash our boobs?"

I have no idea what was going on in my head when I was dating her.

Skip rubs his chin like an old Kung Fu master. "The old

cleavage bomb trick. I like it. How's it going to get you to the bottom?"

Sabrina turns to me. "Maybe some hot guys will carry us down."

Once again, I chastise myself for spending time between those beautiful boobs of hers.

Avery and Preeti categorically refuse to flash their tits.

Skip throws his hands up. "Fuck it. Let's go. I don't give a shit." He whips a joint out of his pocket, lights it, blows a long trail of smoke, coughs three times then speaks again. "We're going to lose, no matter what. Might as well have fun and enjoy this team bonding. And this dank weed."

"Can I get a hit off that?" Jerry asks.

Skip blows smoke in his face. "No."

Malcolm bursts through the door. "I smell smoke."

"Correctamundo." Skip passes the joint to the camp counselor, who then inhales.

Jerry looks wounded.

Where am I? And how did I get here?

On the way to grab my gear, I pass Charlie and her herd of dogs. She purposely bumps me on the stairwell.

"Bet that hurt you more than it did me," I say.

A spasmodic stink-eye flickers. "Know what hurts worse? The bite mark above my left nipple."

"Shove me again, and I'll put one on your thigh." I don't even know why I said that. It just popped out randomly.

Her lips part, and all I can think about is shoving my cock between them.

With my last shred of willpower, I climb the remaining steps and call out behind me, "Stay away from me and neither one of us will get hurt." I turn back. "Again."

"Sick him, Julius. Trippy, kill!" The dogs cock their heads to the side. "God, you guys are useless."

A tiny bit of ice melts from around my heart. God, I miss her. I didn't even realize how much until now.

THIRTEEN

Eli Soars

Eli's Mixtape: Matt & Kim, "Let's Run Away"

January 1999

"You're going to kill yourself," I shouted.

Charlie readied herself to snowboard off the roof.

"Get down, Squirt!" Patrick yelled. "We were just messing with you."

She flipped us the bird then almost fell off. "I'm going to make you eat those words. Tell me girls don't have balls. I'll show you, what a *chicken* I am!"

Patrick paced a path through the foot-deep snow. "Get off, or I'm telling Dad!"

"Go ahead," she shot back. "I'll tell him you and Eli broke into the liquor cabinet."

"You little…Hope you enjoy house arrest." Patrick spun on his heel and stomped back inside.

"Charlie, please," I coaxed. "Don't do this. It's dangerous."

"Move out of the way, Loser, before I clobber you."

I clasped my hands in prayer. "Please, please, don't jump off the roof."

And then she vaulted down the house, launched into the air, did a back flip and landed on her ass.

I rushed to her side. "Are you okay?"

Her tiny fist shot up. "That was amazing! You've got to try it." She brushed the snow off her butt and galloped back up to the roof. "Hurry, before Weiner shows up with my parents. Come on! What are you waiting for? Never knew you were such a wimp."

With my manhood at stake, I had no choice but to climb up there with her.

My heart beat as fast as a hummingbird's.

"On the count of three," she said.

On three, I closed my eyes, flew off of the roof, and landed right on my feet.

She landed face down in a snowdrift.

"You okay?"

She flipped around, her face covered with snow. A dot of blood seeped out from her bottom lip.

"You're bleeding!"

"Am I? Oh, no. Quick, do something. Before my dad gets out here."

I yanked off my gloves and pressed my fingertips along her bottom lip.

Her mouth curled up. "Your hands are so warm."

The sun suddenly beamed down on me through the clouds, and I leaned over and gave her a swift kiss.

Her eyes flashed open.

"I'm sorry." I wiped the coppery taste of her blood off my mouth. "I shouldn't have—"

She grabbed the strings of my hoodie and yanked me back. Her slippery tongue poked through my lips.

Her eyes were closed, but mine were wide open.

I wanted to remember the details of that kiss. The way she

smiled as she pressed her mouth against mine. The way her face relaxed. The way her lips shined. The snowflakes on her eyelashes.

I explored her mouth, the metal over her teeth, the taste of hot chocolate on her breath.

It was as if I were floating off that roof again.

The garage door opened, and we broke apart.

Her dad stormed out. "Pat said you were on the roof?"

She spun around on a pretend board. "It was so awesome. Wasn't it, Elliott?"

"I-uh…" I cringed. "She made me."

Her dad glanced up at our tracks. "How much air did you catch?"

"A billion feet!"

Her dad high-fived her then grew serious. "Don't tell your mother. I mean it."

Patrick grunted his outrage. "She never gets in trouble!"

Mr. Sullivan pointed a stern finger at his son. "Next time you wake me up from the best nap of my life, your little sister better be missing a limb."

He pointed at Charlie. "You bust through my roof, and you'll be wearing those braces for the rest of your life."

Then he did an about face. "Wrap up the stunts and get inside. I assume you're staying for dinner, Elliott?"

"Yes, sir."

I glanced at Charlie. She winked at me, and once again, I felt like I was flying off the roof.

Patrick ping-ponged a look between us. "What's going on?"

She grinned. "Elliott kissed me."

I bet if you saw my face right then, you'd have thought a murderer was on the loose and headed right for me with a cleaver. I thought Patrick was going to beat my ass for sure.

"There are six party pizzas in the freezer, dude," Pat said, unfazed. "I'll split 'em with you."

He thought she was lying.

I scrubbed a shaky hand down my face. "Sounds good. I'm starving."

Charlie waved her fingers. "Bye, Elliott. Thanks for making out with me."

"My pleasure, Chicken."

She snorted. "Right, *I'm* the chicken. You wouldn't have gotten up there if it weren't for me, Loser."

Patrick shook his head and made the cuckoo gesture by his temple. "Don't listen to her. Drain bamage."

On the way back inside, I looked over my shoulder.

She blew me a kiss.

And I grinned for a week straight.

FOURTEEN

Eli Hits The Slopes

ORION	SHIMURA
1	0

Survival Tip: *Stress often brings out the dark side of a person. When planning a group expedition, make sure to carefully select your companions.*

Eli's Mixtape: Benjamin Booker, "Violent Shiver"

BRECKENRIDGE SKI AREA

AT THE BASE of the mountain, Proton's owners outfit everyone with gear and give the novices a mini lesson. Mini, as in a thirty-minute demonstration on how to put on and use the equipment.

This does my coworkers no good. Getting on the chairlift proves to be an exercise in humility.

Orion's team, on the other hand, looks like they just stepped out of a ski magazine. They heckle us the whole time.

After a monumental struggle, the female members of our team finally make it on the lift.

Skip, Jerry, Sam, and I let a few impatient teenagers go then get on two chairs after them.

This is a terrible idea. With the snow, visibility right now is maybe two feet.

It's been ten years since I've done this. What if I blow out my knee again?

My reckless feats as a twenty-one-year-old strike me as completely stupid now that I'm thirty-one. I didn't even wear a helmet back then.

I'm wearing one now, by God.

Heavy, wet snow spills down onto the slopes, suffocating all sound except for my breath blowing against my muffler.

Living in New York, I've gotten used to the noise and pollution. Back in the day, I never would have pictured myself in a huge city. This was it for me. The mountains were my life.

A boarder scrapes an edge on a run below and cuts through the silence. I restrain myself from glancing back at Charlie on the lift behind me.

"This is so lit," Jerry says.

"Jerry, please refrain from using pre-teen slang in my presence," Skip tells him.

Jerry jabs me with an elbow. "Hey, St. James, so you never told us what was up with you and Orion's owner. Why's she such a bitch to you?"

"She's not a bitch."

Three sets of mirrored goggles focus on me, and instantly, I regret defending her.

"St. James?" Skip coaxes. "Have you been cavorting with the enemy?"

I stare ahead without answering.

"Speaking of cavorting with the enemy…" Sam's lips quirk to the side. "Anybody hear that herd of elk mating last night?"

"Was that what that was?" Jerry says. "Thought it was Avery's kid."

"I doubt Avery's kid would yell, 'Fuck me, Eli.'" Skip's delivery is as dry as air.

I hang my head and shake it. "Shit."

They all crack up at my expense, hooting and slapping their thighs.

"Is this your plan to knock out the enemy?" Jerry lets loose a hearty guffaw. "Or should I say, knock up the enemy? Hahaha!"

The usual "Shut it, Jerry," doesn't follow.

My boss pulls out a flask from the inside of his coat, takes a stiff pull, and passes it to me. "Maybe she'll give you a job after we lose."

And with that, the conversation about Charlie ends. Thank God my coworkers know when the joke is past its prime.

We pass the flask around until it's empty and chat about nothing in particular. A light buzz comes trickling in.

The rest of the way, I come to think of us as soldiers in arms, fighting this silly war together.

I miss this—friendship with men. I miss the subtle competitive insults, the lack of drama, and the ease of conversation.

Ever since my buddy, El Love, moved in with his girlfriend Effie, I haven't really hung out with any dudes.

Near the top, we all jerk to attention and watch as our female coworkers approach the landing.

"Dibs on who falls first?" Jerry muses.

"Shut it, Jerry," Skip replies.

There's a struggle and shouting.

I wipe the fog off my goggles. "What the—?"

"Oh, shit," Sam mumbles.

Avery beats the hell out of the lift operator with her ski pole. The poor guy lets go of the chair, and the bench springs up and heads back down the mountain with our team still on board.

"Fffffffff…" Skip continues until they pass us then finally releases the last syllables. "…uuuuuk."

"They didn't get off," Jerry says

"Thanks, Captain Obvious," Sam replies.

Avery waves at us then calls out to Orion's team. "We're beating you!"

My other coworkers cackle like mean girls in high school and glide down the mountain with their middle fingers out.

The Goth chick from Orion's team screams at them. "You filthy, cheating whores!"

"Street rulz, bitch!" Preeti shouts back.

Slight surprise registers on Skip's face. "I'm giving the intern a raise."

"To what?" I say. "A dollar?"

"Worth every penny."

We arrive at the top, and I buckle my chinstrap. "Ready to ride, gentlemen?"

"As ever, you bunch of pussies," Jerry answers.

"Shut it, Jerry," we all say in unison and jump off the lift.

We slide down the mountain like old men.

Except Sam. He flies off the peak in his skis and lands right behind Duffy the Deadhead from the other team. We make fun of him for wearing cross-country skis, and then take off.

Skip passes me on the left. "St. James, why aren't you Olympic athlete-ing your ass down the mountain?"

Jerry screams, "Yee haw!" and passes us with the tips of his skis together, snowplowing like a four-year old, his poles tucked under his armpits.

I turn on the power and go for it. I can't see four feet in front of me, and it's exhilarating.

We hit a dead end, with an option to take a shorter black diamond trail with moguls or a longer blue trail to the bottom. Moguls are hell for boarders.

While we stop to discuss, Orion's team passes us—the skiers jetting down the black and the boarders zooming down the blue.

Sam takes off down the black and the rest of us speed down the blue.

I shift into high gear and pass Joy and Wang. Charlie's a leg ahead.

Skip bursts out of the trees in front of them. "We've got you now, motherfuckers."

I laugh and shoot up my fist. "Yes!"

Now I'm just behind Charlie.

She pulls a sharp left and cuts through the trees.

Wang brakes. "Dude, don't go in there. You'll get stuck."

"Just go," Charlie yells. "Win!"

Skip slides to a stop and bends over, panting. "Altitude's getting to me.

"It's the pot, dude."

"Whatever, why aren't you fleeing after them?"

I stare into the trees.

"Worried about the enemy?"

"It's not safe in there."

He nods. "In that other patch, the drifts were up to my nads. Is it a shortcut?"

"If she makes it out."

He claps me on the back. "Better go see if she needs help."

Skip's growing on me.

I cruise a little further down to where the snow isn't so deep and cut through the trees. Branches whack my helmet as I steer a path to Charlie ahead. "You're going to bury yourself alive!" I shout.

"Chicken!" she shouts back. "Bawk! Bawk!"

There's a crack and a grunt, and I no longer see her. I get stuck in a thicket and have to backtrack to make it out.

Up ahead, she's face down in the snow, not moving, her legs at an awkward angle.

I land next to her and yank off my board.

When I flip her over, there's a giant, snow-covered grin shining up at me.

"You little—I thought you were hurt!"

She blows a raspberry and throws snow in my face. "Still a big fat loser after all these years. You'll never beat me."

I try not to smile. "Did you hurt your shoulder?"

"Nah." She rolls it in demonstration.

We're quiet for a beat. It's uncomfortable. "You know," I say, "I let you win all those times."

"Pfft. Right. Only losers say things like that."

"Think about it for a second. You really think you beat me at snowboarding?"

She sits up and punches her fists in the air. "I am still the master."

"The master-bater."

She falls back and giggles. "I haven't had this much fun in ages. I haven't been snowboarding in years." She licks the snow off her lips. "Are you having fun, despite…us?"

I say nothing.

She lifts her goggles so I can see her eye roll. "You could at least pretend."

I can't help myself; I reach out and brush the snow off her lips.

She frowns. "I miss you, Elliott." Her voice is just an octave above the sound of the snow falling around us. "I've missed you forever."

My chest traps my breath. I lower my hand and don't tell her what I'm thinking. *I miss you, too.*

"Can we be friends again?" She takes my hand and squeezes it.

Why does that feel like a booby prize? I don't want to be her friend. I spent eight years being her friend, and it nearly killed me. Then I spent a year as her boyfriend, and it *did* kill me.

With her, there is no in-between. When it comes to Charlie, friendship isn't an option.

My lack of response enrages her. "You can't even be friends with me?"

I raise my hands. "Hold on! I didn't say that. It's just...dangerous."

She heaves herself out of the drift and flaps her arms. "Dangerous? Dangerous! What? Are you afraid I'm going to leave you in the middle of a crisis? That's your M.O., buddy, not mine." She straps on her board and straightens her helmet.

"Where are you going?"

"To win this race." And then she's gone.

Again.

My skin tingles with heat. I just lost the race for Shimura's team. By caring.

My muscles burn the rest of the ride down. Toward the end of the run, I catch Skip shooting up the side of the super pipe in the snowboard park. Apparently, he's not terribly distraught about losing.

I stop to watch, amazed at how athletic he is. Skip's always struck me as a sedentary guy.

"Nice moves, dude," I tell him when he exits the pipe.

Skip pulls down his muffler and reveals a broad grin.

It creeps me out a little. My boss only smiles when he wants something.

"Man, I haven't boarded since I took over the agency," he says. "Hell, I haven't really been outside since I took over the agency."

"You skate?" I ask.

"Skate, surf, board. This shit's like my religion." He inhales the air.

"Me too, man. I miss it."

"Look me up in the city. I'll skate with you." He drops the subject and picks up another. "You save hot toddy?"

"Yeah, then she took off and left me."

"Ungrateful wench. Might as well ride then."

We take a couple more runs down the pipe and just as we gear up to leave, Deadhead Duffy appears with his skis over his shoulder, his ponytail whipping in the wind. He waves. "Broke my binding."

"Sucks, man," I say. "Want to ride down on the back of my board?"

Duffy jogs over. "Thanks, man."

Skip takes his skis and poles, and Orion's copywriter climbs on the back of my board and grips my shoulders.

"Oh, you're so strong," he jokes in an effeminate voice.

I cut him a look. "Want a ride or not?"

He laughs. "Ride on, stallion."

We coast down the mountain to the bottom. It's a short ride, but a serious pain-in-the-ass. At the end, Duffy jumps off my board and runs like hell to the bar, leaving Skip and me still holding his equipment.

"That son-of-a-dirty-snatched-pony-tailed bitch," Skip says with the usual desert-dry tone.

"Seriously, what a thunder cunt," I add.

Skip drops Duffy's gear in the snow. "Hey, what did the Deadhead say when he ran out of weed?"

"No idea."

"This music sucks."

I don't laugh. "Second time today I've helped someone only to be screwed over."

My boss pulls off his helmet and goggles. "What do you think, St. James? Think we should just clear out of here and fly home? Is this just a big waste of time?"

There's that weird pinch in my gut again. "Nah, man. Can't give up now."

Skip blows out a breath. "I'm just gonna pretend I'm on vacation."

"Good plan."

"Let's go get drunk."

"Another good plan."

Inside the bar, it's warm and cozy and smells like winter. The snow drips off my beard as I take in the scene. I used to love this place. It's done up like an old cabin, with six different rooms, some with couches, some with tables, another with a bar.

Everyone has goggle marks and helmet heads and red noses and wind-burned cheeks.

The Proton camp is seated in the room with the fireplace. Several pitchers of beer are scattered across the table.

Avery rocks back in her chair with her son in her lap. "How is it that the fastest snowboarder among us came in dead last?"

I scoot up a chair next to her and pour myself a beer.

"St. James was too busy saving Orion's team," Skip informs her.

Wang interrupts. "A real man doesn't blame others for his defeat."

Skip gulps down his beer and burps. "You know, Wang"—he draws out the Wang—"Japan beat the shit out of China in WWII."

"No, they didn't."

"Yeah, well, we had a cooler flag."

"The Japanese flag looks like a butthole," Wang retorts.

"Your face was the inspiration."

Avery's kid blurts out, "Butthole," and dies laughing.

The left side of my body heats up. I turn to face the culprit.

Charlie's glaring at me again. Her messy hair is bunched on the top of her head, pieces of it falling around her hilarious bitch face.

I rub my beard to cover my smile.

She attempts another snarl, and I pop out a half-grin.

That infuriates her, and in a huff, she storms off.

I finish my beer, take a couple of digs at Duffy, and then casually wander off to find her.

By the way, my body is doing this on its own accord. It's not my brain's idea to chase after her.

Buddha crosses my mind. I should really let this go. I ignore him. The guy was celibate; therefore his advice is null and void.

I spot her headed for the bathroom. Right before she closes

the door, I wedge my foot in, slipping inside and locking the door behind me.

Hands on hips and eyes narrowed to a crack, she silently seethes.

Trust me. It's hot.

"What do you think you're doing?"

"Claiming my reward for saving your ass."

She softens. "Thank you. But I didn't need your help."

I grab her by the waist. "What *do* you need?"

She grabs my collar. "You. But you said you didn't want to be friends."

"I don't."

She releases her grip and bites her bottom lip. "Then what *do* you want?" Her voice is soft and delicate.

"You're pretty cute when you're not so pissed off."

"And when I am?"

"Hot as fuck."

She grabs my face and gives me a violent kiss.

I nibble her neck. "I never wanted to be your friend, Chicken."

"Then don't be." Her voice is a breathless whisper.

I shove her sweater up and latch onto her nipple. While I suck and nibble that one, I pluck and pull the other one.

"Your hands are cold."

I smile and look at her. "Your tits are warm."

She gives me a half-lidded lusty glare and runs a hand down the front of my pants. "I want to see that smug smirk between my thighs."

I chuckle. "You actually think I'm going to service you after that stunt in the trees?"

She unzips my pants and pulls out my stiff cock. Her teeth graze my chin. "I want to feel those whiskers on my pussy."

Whoosh! There goes my control, right down the toilet.

In one move, I shove down her pants and trace a finger down her wet seam.

She tugs my collar again. "I'm warning you. If you don't make me come, you won't live to see the sunset."

My touch is light, my fingertips hovering above her clit, feathering caresses above the hard ridge. "Someone's awfully wet. How long have you been like this? Since you left my ass in the trees?"

"I mean it." Her voice is soft, but her grip on my dick is hard.

I grunt and shove my cock into her tight fist, then sink a finger inside her slick cunt.

She bites my nipple through my flannel and squirms over my hand.

Another finger inserted.

Another tight jerk on my cock.

Her juices coat my hand as I work that pussy exactly like I remember, until she's shivering, swaying, and moaning sounds of pure delight.

I perfected my moves on her a long time ago, getting the rhythm just right for this response.

Judging by her parted lips, half-lidded gaze, and frantic bounce, she's almost there.

I bring another hand into the game and stroke her clit.

Her legs tremble, and her body stills. Then she lets out a long panting moan and slumps against me.

My turn. I thrust hard into her loosening grip. I curl my fingers around hers and pump.

I'm mere seconds away from creaming all over her when someone bangs on the door.

"Charlotte? Are you in there?" It's that douchebag, Alan.

"Yeah?" she squeaks.

"You okay? You've been in there for a while."

My dick wilts.

"Sorry," she mouths silently to me. "I'm fine, Al. Just feeling a little lightheaded."

He raps again. "Let me in."

She pulls up her pants and fixes her shirt. "No! Go away, Alan. I'm fine."

"Okay, text if you need me."

I no longer feel like feel like coming. I feel like punching.

His footsteps shuffle off, and we stand in front of the mirror, side-by-side.

I turn to the sink and wash up. When I try to dry my hands, the paper towel comes out in shreds. "Shit." I slam the handle and yank out more useless slivers. "Fuck."

She reaches around me and waves a hand in front of the sensor. A perfect sheet slides out.

"What's with that guy?" I ask. "If you're dating him, why are you in here with me?"

"You followed me here." She sighs. "What are you doing, Elliott?"

I rub a hand over the dull ache in my chest. "I don't know."

She massages the back of her shoulder.

I caress the spot she's touching. "Did I hurt you?"

She flicks me off. "When are you going to talk to me? Really talk to me. About what happened?"

Oh, sure! Let's break it down right now. Let's chat about how I killed your whole family, and you cheated on me and then I left, and now I'm feeling you up ten years later in the fucking john.

The ache spreads to my back. I heave out a breath and rub my fists in my eyes. "What's the point?"

Her pink post-coital glow mutates to red rage. "You coward."

I double over like I've been shot by a sniper's bullet. "What do you want from me, Charlotte?"

She marches off to a stall and slams the door. "Nothing!" A second later she pops it open and glares at me. "Maybe another orgasm. That was fucking hot, until you ruined it."

Immensely relieved by this quick change in subject, I strut to the door. "Next one is on you."

FIFTEEN

Charlie Loses Her Cherry

September 2002

ELI TOOK me to his parent's cabin for the weekend, and he finally, FINALLY, made love to me. Now, every time I look at him out of the corner of my eye he gets this unstoppable smile.

My favorite part was afterward, when he threw me over his shoulder and ran naked around the room, smacking my butt and shouting, "I want to make sure I can save your life when the time comes."

Later at dinner, I confessed my diabolical plan to get him in the sack. I thought he'd be mad, but he welled up with tears and thanked God.

I love him.

SIXTEEN

Charlie Fakes A Smile

Eli's Mixtape: Killavesi, "Unlikely"

MY JAWS ACHE from the plastic smile I've worn for hours. After my public bathroom orgasm, you'd think I'd be grinning for real.

I'm not.

I've been pretending to read a book by the fire for over an hour. What I've really been doing is cataloging my life.

Every sexual experience I've had since Elliott, has left me feeling unsatisfied and full of shame. Why don't I feel like that now?

I come to a sad conclusion—it's because he knows me.

To him, I'm beautiful. He doesn't even have to say it. It's the way he looks at me, like I'm a priceless object, even though he's seen me at my worst. He was there during my awkward teenage years. He's seen me sick as a dog and drowning with grief. He was with me when I got my first period.

Only with him have I ever felt comfortable enough to make ugly "O" faces and let loose.

I look over at him. Sabrina, who's hanging on his every word, shrieks out a laugh.

I can't be around them for one more second.

Quietly, I slip on my boots and sneak out the door with the dogs.

Snow flutters to the earth like goose down as I make my way to the dock.

All at once, I can't hold it in anymore. Warm tears flow down my frozen cheeks and cling to the fur around my hood.

What is wrong with me?

I haven't cried in years. But in the last few days, I've shed tears at least twenty times.

I'm shivering violently. My body has no idea what to do with all this emotion.

Julius Seizure paws my leg.

"Maybe I should adopt another dog," I tell him, scrubbing behind his ears.

Thom Yorkie yaps, and I pick him up and tuck him inside my jacket. Instantly, his Frito smell comforts me.

Orion shines down from a clear patch of black in the sky. "Dad?" I whisper. "Are you there? I've got boy problems."

I laugh like a gust of wind.

What the hell am I doing? Talking to my dead father? This isn't me.

Elliott has me all flustered.

I trudge back to the lodge. Inside, it's dark except for the few glowing embers in the fireplace. I shrug off my coat and warm my hands.

"I was worried about you."

I flinch and spin.

Alan's on the couch with a brandy snifter.

"How long have you been there?" I ask.

"Since you left. I was about to join you out by the lake, but I could tell something was on your mind."

He's not the one I want to care. "Just needed some alone time. I'm not used to living around a bunch of people."

He swirls the drink, his gaze as hard as the dark liquor in his glass. "Were you thinking"—he pauses—"about us?"

The question rams a thousand pound ball of lint down my throat. I say nothing.

Then he punches me again. "Is something going on between you and that Eli guy?"

I lunge for the bottle of brandy on the table and take a hearty swig. "Woo! That lit a fire in me."

His mouth tics up then falls flat. "Sit next to me." He pats the cushion. "I miss your smell."

I down more brandy and completely ignore his comment. "Looks like we're going to win this business, partner."

"Does that make you happy?" he asks.

Not really. "Of course."

He stares into space for a second.

"Something on your mind, buddy?" I emphasize the buddy.

"You're on my mind. All the time." He sounds tortured.

I'm trapped. If I kick him to the curb now, in the middle of these games, it would be an unmitigated disaster.

Why can't he get the frickin' hint? He probably thinks I want him to chase me. *Men are so stupid.*

"Al," I say after a long silence.

"Char."

"I don't do this…" I wave a hand between us. "I told you that."

He places a hand on my cheek. It feels like bat wings. "I can take care of you, Charlotte."

Just tell him. Tell him you don't want him. Spit it out. But the words get stuck in my throat. I can't do this right now. How can I be so cruel to a man who's been so good to me?

Why, oh, why can't I fall in love with a good guy like Alan?

"I'm sorry," is all I manage to say. "I'm not…relationship material."

His demeanor turns to marble. Without a word, he sets down his glass and staggers off to his room.

I know how he feels. The person I loved rejected me, too.

But once I'm in bed, I barely give him a second thought.

My mind is on the big blond man two doors down. There just isn't any room for anyone else in my brain. Elliott takes up too much space.

SEVENTEEN

Charlie Cheers for a Loser

February 2000

ELLIOTT JUST BEAT the world record in racing. If this keeps up, he's going to get a big head and forget about me.

Last night, I made a sign with rainbows and glitter that said "Go Loser," and I held it up the end of the finish line.

I think that's what made him go faster. I'm a genius.

EIGHTEEN

Charlie Makes a Hard Dick

ORION	SHIMURA
2	0

Eli's Mixtape: Sweet, "Blockbuster"

THE WORLD LOOKS like a giant white pillow outside the lodge. The agencies stand across from each other, in the field next to the lake, while Burt delivers the rules of the next game.

"First half of the morning, your teams will build a snow fort. You will be judged on the design and strength of the fort," he says. "The second half of the day, we'll play a modified game of capture the flag. First team to capture the most flags and tear down the opponents' fort with snow weaponry wins—"

Sabrina raises her hand. "What's snow weaponry?"

Skip yanks her arm down. "We've got it, Burt, thanks."

My godfather gives everyone a crinkly-eyed smile. "You have one hour. Then we'll break for lunch and have us a snowball fight."

Art grins demonically next to him and dips his shades. "Bonus points for creativity." Then the two walk arm-in-arm back to the lodge, laughing like hyenas.

I glance at Elliott. He's deep in conversation with his team.

Everyone on mine looks bored.

"All right, people!" I shout. "We are undefeated, untouchable, unstoppable and—"

"Unsterile." Joy nods to Wang.

"Joy." I shake a finger at her. "Would you please be serious for a moment?"

"When am I not serious? He's got a dirty dick."

Alan speaks up. "Let's not discuss genital hygiene on the job."

"Yes, let's not talk about your filthy premarital sex lives in front of Jesus," Christine says.

We all stop and stare at her.

Joy rolls her eyes. "Fine. What do we do about this igloo?"

Exhausted from lack of sleep, I'm sorely tempted to tell my team to make a pile of snow and call it a day.

Wang pulls a calculator out of his jacket and punches in some numbers.

Stanley snorts. "What kind of geek brings a calculator outside?"

"A geek who got 700 on the SATs and a full ride to Harvard."

Joy snickers. "Why the hell are you in advertising, then? In Denver, no less."

"Because my mom's sick and she needs help with my little sisters."

Joy's smugness stalls out. "You never told me that."

"You never asked."

"The clock is ticking, dudes," Duffy points out.

I shout my orders. "Start shoveling!"

"We need water to pack the snow. This powder isn't going to hold," Wang tells us, as if he's the authority on snow forts.

I grab a bucket and head to the hot tub.

Someone closes in behind me.

"You're gonna fall in," says a sexy, gruff voice.

I whip around and see Elliott. He's like a radiator, the way he heats up my body.

"Mind your own business, Loser." I turn my back on him and fill up the pail. Once the task is done, I muster up my intimidating look.

His lips twitch then he doubles over and laughs.

I feel violent all of a sudden. "Am I amusing you?"

He muffles a snort behind his hand. "It's just…" He bends over again. "You should see your face."

I push past him, sloshing water everywhere.

"Let me get that for you," he says.

"Go away!"

"Charlie, let me help you."

Alan lunges for me. "Need some help, babe?" he says. "Don't want you to strain your shoulder."

Elliott's fists clench as if he's preparing for a battle.

A slight groan escapes my tight jaw. "Don't call me babe, Alan." I desperately need to rid myself of this albatross coworker of mine.

But also, I need to win.

Snorting and grunting like a wooly mammoth, I lumber back to our fort, spilling half the bucket on the way.

Shimura's fort is coming along.

Ours has barely begun.

"What is the hold up, Wang?" I shout.

"Hush!" His brow is furrowed in deep concentration. "You can't rush perfection."

"What do you want me to do?"

"Get down," he shouts. "You're going to cave this thing in."

"Wang!"

"Go!"

Never put a perfectionist in charge of building a snow fort.

We need a backup plan in case this fails. I need female brains to save us from this catastrophe. "Christine, Joy. Get over here."

Laughs erupt from the other side.

I tear off my jacket and start ordering them to build my vision. "Chop! Chop! Christine. Work those muscles."

Halfway through, my receptionist figures out what we're building. "I want no part of this profanity."

Joy scoffs. "Is it painful?"

"Is what painful?" Christine asks.

"That big stick in your ass?"

Duffy chuckles then ducks behind the pagoda, which is still nowhere close to being done.

I tilt my head back and try to blind myself with the sun. What would the CEO of Grayson Advertising say if he saw me now? I'll tell you what he'd say. "You're cracking, Charlotte."

Because I am.

I take a deep breath. "Christine, if you could perhaps put aside your delicate sensibilities and take one for the team, I'd really appreciate it."

My receptionist frowns and strokes her cross for another moment, then goes back to work.

In the meantime, Proton sets up a folding table with industrial-sized canisters of hot, spiked cider.

I almost drop to my knees like Christine and give thanks to Jesus.

Art blows a whistle. "Time's up!"

"Great," Duffy grumbles. "We don't even have a roof."

"Should have built a simple igloo," Stanley laments.

"It's impenetrable," Wang shoots back.

"Like your cold, dead heart," Joy mumbles.

I scurry over to the table and hold out my Styrofoam cup for Malcolm. "All the way to the top. I mean it."

While I'm guzzling the scorching hot drink, Proton tours the forts, whispering and marking things off on an official-looking clipboard. They deliberate for a few more minutes then blow the whistle again.

I'm going to strangle him with that thing, if he doesn't quit blowing it.

"Looks like we have a tie this round," Art says.

Avery cries, "They didn't even finish!"

I'm as shocked as she is.

"Look again." Malcolm points to our sculpture off to the side. "The penis hut is finished. We took off a point, because it will only hold a small child, but nevertheless it's still a fort. And it's creative."

Skip's arms fly out. "For fuck's sake."

I send a suspicious glance over to Art.

He shrugs.

Why is he doing this? Why not just cut Shimura loose? Hell, why not cut me loose?

I ponder this for four more ciders, and then stop caring on the fifth.

NINETEEN

Eli Kicks A Dog

Survival Tip*: If a collision seems inevitable, stay with it, and if possible, drive into something soft. If this option isn't available, brace yourself.*

Eli's Mixtape: Soft Cell, "Tainted Love"

HYPERSEXUAL RADIATION BEAMS out from Charlie's bronze orbs throughout lunch.
    At least I think that's what it is. I'm kind of drunk off that cider. Everyone is.
    That tool, Alan, is staring at her with the same burn.
    I wad my napkin into the shape of a bullet and watch him watch her stroll to the kitchen.
    Her little dog stays behind and barks at him. First he checks to see if anyone's looking, then he gives the mutt a swift kick.
    In no time, I'm in his face, fisting his stupid sweater and shoving him against the wall. "You little shit. I see you hurt an innocent animal again, and I'll hurt you."

I let go, and he slumps to the floor.

"What are you talking about? I didn't kick her dog."

I shove my foot in his ass and stomp off.

My edginess is coming back with a vengeance. I'm off-kilter, like blood is pumping through my arteries at an unnatural rate.

This feeling, like the earth is moving under my feet? I've felt it a dozen times before. The common denominator is always Charlie.

TWENTY

Eli Gets A Tattoo

Boulder, Colorado, 2004

ONE BRIGHT BLUE AUTUMN MORNING, Patrick and I were happily eating brunch at a cafe on Pearl Street, when Charlie and her roommate breezed by our table and wrecked my entire life.

"Squirt!" Patrick called out to his sister.

The girls spun around and sat down at our table.

Something was off about Charlie that day. She wouldn't look me in the eye.

Patrick seemed equally puzzled. He pinched his sister's cheek. "What's up, dudette? Hungover?"

Whilst browsing the menu, her roommate casually announced, "She's sore from a night of hot sex."

My hand jerked out and knocked over my Bloody Mary.

Patrick dropped his fork on his plate with a loud clang. "What the fuck do you mean, you're sore?"

"Yeah, what do you fucking mean, you're sore?" I said.

Charlie punched her friend's shoulder so hard the girl fell out of her seat.

Once she got back in her chair, her roommate lifted a glass. "Shall we have a toast? To your sister's womanhood?" She glanced at me and quickly lowered the glass. "Never mind."

It must have looked like I'd been punched in the nuts. Because I had been.

Patrick knocked down Charlie's menu. "What is she talking about?"

"So what did you guys have?" Charlie asked. "I'm thinking about the eggs Benedict."

Oh, you mean the breakfast that's about to burst out of my mouth? No, as a matter of fact, it tastes a lot like burning betrayal.

Someone had popped her cherry. Someone besides me. I covered my mouth as the nightmarish scene played through my mind—Charlie in bed with another man.

I retched and coughed.

Patrick stood. "I need a minute," he said and stormed out of the restaurant.

Her roommate's phone rang. "Yo! I can't hear you. Let me go outside."

All of a sudden it was just the Scarlet Letter and I.

"Who was it?" My voice cracked like a prepubescent boy.

She didn't look up from her menu. "Huh?"

I grabbed it out of her hands and flung it aside. "Who did you fuck last night?"

She lifted her chin. "What do you care? You don't want anything to do with me."

I replied through clenched teeth, "I can't have anything to do with you, because your brother won't let me."

She shrugged and picked up her roommate's menu. "Well, then, that's too bad."

"Did he hurt you?"

"It wasn't exactly paradise, but I'm sure it will get better with practice."

I threw the menu on the other table. "With practice!"

"Well, yeah. Where are you going?"

Somewhere far away from you. I grabbed my skateboard and blasted outside, cruising down Pearl Street at Mach 10 speed, not caring one bit if I slammed into a pole.

And then I saw it. The only thing that could take away my pain. A tattoo parlor.

During the five hours of stabbing pain, I took a long, hard look at my friendship with Charlie's brother.

All my firsts were with him. First porn viewing. First time getting drunk. First backpacking adventure. First time snowboarding. In fact, he was the one who got me into racing.

And Patrick's family was more important than my own. They were my support system. They went to all my races. They celebrated my birthdays like I was their kid. My own mother was too busy cheating on my dad, and my dad was too busy working.

I loved Patrick. I loved his parents. And I loved Charlie. Why couldn't I have all of them?

For years, Patrick told me I was too slutty for her. I should have told him I was slutty *because* of her. Because he wouldn't let me be with her.

I tried to find someone else. Someone as challenging as her. And it didn't work. And then she went and fucked someone else.

The tattoo artist was a burly biker dude, or I'd have cried right there with the needle in my arm.

If my best friend couldn't accept that I was in love with his sister, then I'd just have to go behind his back.

Eventually, he'd come to terms with it. Especially when he saw how much I loved her. And one day, maybe during the holidays, we'd all sit around the table and laugh at how stupid this was.

Once the tattoo was done, I rushed to Charlie's dorm and threw a rock at her window. It crashed through the glass. "Charlie!"

Her head popped into view. "What the hell!"

"Let me in!"

The buzzer sounded at the main entrance, and I took the stairs two at a time up to her room.

She was standing in the doorway, looking furious. "You're going to pay for that."

"Is your roommate here?"

"No. Why?"

I pushed past her and entered her dorm. Then I grabbed her by the waist and folded her into my arms. "You are mine. Do you hear me? Mine."

She licked her lips and nodded.

I clutched the back of her neck and gave her a greedy kiss that was both rough and sweet.

She melted in my arms like snow on warm ground.

I pressed my forehead against hers. "It should have been me."

Her hands gripped my biceps, and I jerked back out of her grip.

Her brows lowered. "Did I hurt you?"

I unzipped my hoodie and showed her my arm.

She moved in for a closer look. "You got a tattoo? Of feathers?"

"Chicken feathers. For you."

Her arm swung in front of her stomach, and she bent over and guffawed.

"You don't like it?"

"Oh, Elliott." She caressed my face. "You adorable man. You defaced your beautiful body for me, with"—she snorted and doubled over again—"chicken feathers! When you're old and withered, you are so going to regret this."

"Not as much as I regret letting another man steal your virginity."

Her laughter faded. "I wish I could grow it back for you. I didn't think you wanted me."

I shook my head and yanked her pigtail. "I've always wanted you."

"What about Patrick?"

"Screw him."

"Really?"

"No. We'll have to keep this a secret. For now."

She sighed. "Okay, but not for long. I don't like lying to my family."

"I have to go to training. Don't make plans this weekend."

"Why?"

"Because I'm going to show you what paradise is."

Her roommate kicked open the door right then, and unloaded a case of Mountain Dew on the floor. "Dudes! I'm cracked out on caffeine. Anyone want to run a marathon?"

I zipped up my hoodie. "Walk me to the door, Chicken."

"When are you going to stop calling me that?"

"Never."

The door slammed shut then opened again.

"Next time, Loser," she shouted down the hallway, "don't make me wait. Also, you owe me for that window."

Later, I found out she'd made up the entire story to get me into bed. I've never been so happy to have a woman lie to me.

❅

Eli's Mixtape: The Romantics, "What I Like About You"

SINCE ORION'S pagoda melted into a pile of nothing over lunch, the only thing of theirs left to topple was the dick hut.

In less than ten minutes, we lob the head off of it. We follow that up with an endless amount of shit giving.

The defeat is huge. We're tied.

While we're hugging it out and high-fiving each other, our enemies bolt into the woods with red flags Velcroed to their waists.

"Game's not over, team," Skip says, like a general at war.

"What's the plan?" asks Sabrina. "Should we chase after them?"

"Personally, I'm gonna smoke a fatty." Skip waves a hand. "But chase away, if that's what you want."

"Make sure to flash your boobs," Sam tells Sabrina with a poker face.

Preeti looks horrified. "That religious woman will call the police."

"Not a good idea," Avery says, grabbing Skip's joint and taking a toke.

"Adams! I'm shocked," he says, not sounding the slightest bit shocked.

"Get over it." She takes a hit and blows smoke in his face. "My kid's asleep. I'm having fun. Might as well smoke a doob."

"I have a bong in my room."

I groan. "Are we going to stand here and get high? Or are we going to beat these clowns?" I can't wait to see Charlie's face when we win. Revenge will be so delicious.

Skip pinches the end of the joint, stuffs it back in his pocket, then wanders off in the opposite direction.

"Useless," I mutter. "Guess it's up to us, guys."

No one moves.

"Fischer?"

"I'm in," he says.

Together, we head into the woods like a medieval huntsman. My first target? Alan. And after I take him down, I'm taking Charlie. And I'm not talking about her flags.

With Sam by my side, we crouch to examine footprints like we're Cheyenne scouts. It's ludicrous, and we laugh the whole way.

Sam caws like a bird then throws a two-finger signal behind a tree.

I leap up like a rabbit and take Alan by surprise.

The tool chuckles and raises his hand. "Got me, man."

Damn right I did. Now go away.

Off to the side, a set of dog prints meander deep into the forest. I stuff the flags in my pocket and motion to Sam. With a few far-fetched military signals, I more or less tell him it's time to split up.

Somehow he understands me and breaks left.

The footprints end at the bottom of tree, where the four beasts lay protectively around the trunk.

I look up, and WHAM! Charlie jumps out of the tree, lands on top of me, and rips off my flags.

The wind is knocked out of me, and while I'm still trying to catch a breath, she straddles my chest and grins like an evil elf.

"How'd you climb up there with your shoulder?"

"Never-you-mind."

"You could have broken something."

"Hmpf. You're the one grunting like an old man."

I flip her over on her back. While she squirms underneath me, I tear my flags from her hands then grab hers and stuff them down my pants.

One of her dogs toddles over and sniffs me. "I'm not hurting her, boy." I wiggle my brows. "Yet."

She thrashes under me. "Get off!"

I yank my gloves off with my teeth, unzip her jacket and shove my hands under her sweater. Her nipples pucker delightfully. "Ah, warm and toasty under there."

She tears at my zipper. "Gimme those flags."

I sit up and put my knees on either side of her chest. "Take 'em. And while you're there…" More brow wiggles ensue.

Her body stills. "What are you doing?"

"Pinching your nipples."

"I know that! But what are you doing? Why do you keep doing this?"

"Pinching your nipples?"

Her lips clamp together as if she's fighting not to enjoy it.

I unzip my pants the whole way. "Time to claim my prize," I joke. "Open up, Chicken."

Never in a million years did I think she'd grab my cock and swallow me whole.

"Whoa. Yeah. Okay. Do it."

Her teeth gently scrape my head while her tongue swirls and sucks down my length. She moans, closes her eyes, and savors my cock like it's the most wonderful thing in the world.

It is.

Her warm fingers curl around my balls and tug. The cold outside and the heat inside her mouth—it's so painfully good.

I reach back, unzip her snow pants, and bury my cold fingers in her hot, slick warmth.

Again she moans.

I'm in the midst of getting a backwoods BJ by a beautiful woman. Time for some dirty talk. "Suck it," I coax. "Suck it hard. You look so good sucking my cock." I pump a few times then concentrate on her needs, because rubbing her clit turns me on as much as her lips on my dick.

It's building rather quickly. "I don't know how much longer I can hold off," I say.

She looks up at me. *I need you, I want you, I miss you, I'm hungry for you*, she says with her eyes.

Translation not necessary—I'm telling her the same things.

I tilt my head back and stop breathing.

Grunting and panting, I tense, jerk my base, and shoot a hot load down her throat. Cum pulses out of me at an alarming rate. "Drink my dick, beautiful," I tell her. "That's it."

A drop dribbles out of the side of her lip. I capture it with my pussy-drenched finger and let her suck it off.

"That was incredible. I should win more often."

She kisses my tip and gives me sultry kitty side-eye. "You've gotten dirty in your old age."

"I've always been dirty." I zip up my pants.

Deep and hard, I kiss her, tasting myself on her tongue.

But it doesn't feel like a kiss. It feels much worse. I'm falling for her again.

A stick cracks, and her littlest dog barks.

I roll off of her.

The sound of bickering nears. Joy and Wang appear and freeze in their tracks.

Charlie stumbles to her feet and brushes the snow off her clothes. "Hey, guys."

They tilt their heads in the same direction.

"What are you doing?" Joy asks.

I yank a flag from my pants. "I'm fucking your boss."

Charlie gasps then chuckles. "He's kidding."

While they're gaping, I tear off Joy and Wang's flags and saunter off.

"Not cool!" Wang blusters.

"Street rulz, bitch." I laugh like a madman all the way back to the lodge.

No, really, I'm going crazy. This adventure, Charlie, this stupid fresh mountain air, the fun—I'm losing my ever-loving mind.

I need to meditate.

My team is milling around the fort when I arrive. I hold six flags over my head. "Lookie what I got."

Sabrina sprints over and jumps in my arms. I briefly consider dropping her on her ass. Instead, I loosen my grip and lower her to her feet.

Her smile unfolds into a disappointed frown.

Sam holds up six more flags.

Jerry whips two more over his head like a lasso.

Avery throws another two flags in the air and lets them float to the ground.

"We won?" I ask. "For real?" I mean I feel like a winner after that backwoods BJ, but I didn't expect to actually *win* the game.

"Fischer's military training paid off," Skip says. "Our brilliant developer camouflaged himself with a white trash bag and ambushed them." He lets out one "Ha!"

I fist-bump Sam. "Way to go, dude."

Avery giggles obscenely.

Skip throws a glance over his shoulder and then shows us his contraband phone. "Got it all on video. I'm going to post it on the company blog."

"Hell, yeah!" Jerry tries to fist bump my boss.

Skip gives him a blank stare in return.

"So we're tied with Orion?" I ask.

"Here's to beating Orion's arse!" Preeti staggers over with a cup of cider in her hand. "We now have a good chance of winning the business."

"The intern is wasted," Skip informs me.

"Highly intoxifuckcated," she says.

I laugh and give her a hug.

Then, like a little league team that just won a pennant, we lift our boss on our shoulders and carry him to the lodge, shouting, "Shimura! Shimura!"

Is it too soon to admit this is the best goddamned business trip ever?

TWENTY-ONE

Charlie Is Tired of Waiting

December 2003

IF ONE MORE OF Elliott's playthings asks me if I'm his sister, I'm going to go postal.

Why does he keep this up? I know he doesn't want to be with any of these girls.

I talked to Weiner about it. He says Elliott needs to man up and ask me out. But until that happens, he's going to give him eternal shit.

I feel sorry for those girls. I feel sorry for me.

Stupid loser.

Later that week

Today was a sad day. Sir Farts A Lot passed away. Elliott dug a hole in the frozen ground in our backyard. It took him two hours, but he said he wanted to make sure the hole was deep enough. He lined it with my dog's favorite blanket and bought flowers and everything. I don't think I've ever felt so sad. How can people bear to lose their loved ones, when I can barely deal with losing my old dog?

RIP boy.

TWENTY-TWO

Charlie Has A Fit

ORION	SHIMURA
2	2

Eli's Mixtape: Marian Hill, "Down"

LOOK AT HIM, smirking while he eats. Smug, sexy bastard.

These dinners with him are better than the latest fad diet. I don't think I've eaten a full plate of food in days.

He's the one I want to eat up. He's like a potent aphrodisiac. All he has to do is sit there, and I want him.

And why? Why, after all that happened, would I still want that jerk?

Stanley and Wang strike up a conversation with him about his racing days.

If only I could disappear into thin air.

"So if you hadn't blown out your knee," Wang asks, "you would have been one of the first snowboarders in the Olympics?"

Elliott stirs his food around on his plate. "Yep."

"Sucks, man," Stanley says. "All that training for nothing."

"You must have been devastated," Avery adds.

"Nah. Not really."

"Unbelievable," I mutter. Guess he's blocked out that little memory too. He didn't get out of bed for a week.

All eyes land on me.

Alan clears his throat. "Do you guys know each other?"

"Never met the guy," I say without looking up from my plate. He's not the one I fell in love with years ago. Not that cold bastard across from me. I shovel salad into my mouth and crunch down hard.

Burt, seated at the head of the table, chimes in. "I'm pretty sure Beaver Beard was crying like a baby."

Eli tips his beer to Burt and gives him a tight smile. "And how would you know?"

Art lays his hand over Burt's to shut him up.

"What?" Burt asks innocently.

"Let's not insult the guests."

"Nah, I like it," says Elliott. "It's a compliment. I earned that title. Can I get it embroidered on the back of a T-shirt?"

"You should," Sabrina says. "Best ride of my life."

Would anyone mind if I barfed right here? I rest my chin in my hand. "Oh, do tell, Sabrina," I say sarcastically, then realize too late she doesn't understand sarcasm.

"I used to call him magic mouth, didn't I, Eli?"

Eli pinches the bridge of his nose.

Sam tosses his napkin on his plate. "I'm out."

"I second that," Skip says.

Jerry folds his hand across his chest. "I'm in."

"This is inappropriate dinner conversation." Christine gets up from her chair mumbling a verse from the Bible about sodomy and wine.

Sabrina winces. "Guess I let the cat out of the backpack, didn't I?"

"We're all ears, Sabrina," I say.

Elliott shifts in his seat. "No, we're not."

Rather than detail the "incredible head" he gives her, Sabrina pours out their relationship problems. "He wouldn't even introduce me to his roommate. Told me he wanted to keep things a *secret*." She finger quotes secret.

I cross one leg over the other and sit back. "Funny, I dated someone like that. Dated him for a year in secret. He refused to tell anyone, even my family."

The veins in his arms pop as he repeatedly clenches and releases his fists.

"He had all those groupies all over him at the clubs," Sabrina babbles on. "He didn't tell them we were dating."

"That's because we weren't," he says.

Sabrina drinks down her last drop of wine and continues humiliating herself. "I tried to make him jealous." Her lip quivered. "I thought he'd, like, I don't know, make a commitment. But the Saint doesn't like games. 'I don't like games,' he told me."

I narrow my eyes. "Interesting. He strikes me as someone who loves games. Enjoys jerking women around."

"Oh, no," Sabrina slurs. "He hates them."

"That's enough," he says.

I protest. "No, do go on. I love hearing about people's failed relationships. Makes me feel better about my own."

Alan's hand drops to my thigh.

I flick it off.

Art's chair scrapes the floor. "Would you kids like some pie?"

"I'd love some, with whipped cream if you have it," Jerry says.

"Shut it, Jerry," Eli snaps.

"I could use a little wine," I say and pass my empty glass to Art.

He fills it to the brim. Such an amazing godfather, that man.

Elliott pushes away his plate. "Time for bed."

"So soon?" I give him a mocking smile. "It's only eight o'clock. I was hoping to hear more about your magic mouth."

His eyes scrunch at the corners. "I'll tell you all about it later."

I swallow my wine in three gulps. "Well, that was fun."

In actuality, that conversation topped my list of the worst conversations ever, coming in a close second to the one I had with the police the night my whole family died.

Sabrina sighs and watches him leave. "Thank you for listening, everyone. This has been so hard, being around him like this."

I clench my fists under the table. "I completely understand."

Alan holds up the bottle. "More wine, Char?"

If this is his attempt to get me drunk, too late. "No, thanks," I say and whistle for the dogs. "I'm going to bed."

Upstairs, right before I close my door, Eli sticks his boot in the way. I slam the door on his foot a few times until he pushes it open and enters my room.

"Get out," I tell him.

Instead, he locks the door.

His hands jam inside his pockets. "I'm sorry. About Sabrina. She's…" He shakes his head. "Obsessed."

I wave a hand. "No need to apologize. I looooove hearing about your sexual escapades. They sound frighteningly similar to my own."

His lip folds under his teeth.

"Is there anything else?" I fake yawn. "Because I am beat. All that dick sucking really took it out of me."

"Chicken." He takes a step closer and puts a hand on my cheek. "You're not jealous, are you?"

I duck out from under him. "No! We are not doing this again. I had a lapse of judgment. Or three. Game over. I'm done." I point to the door. "Time for you to leave."

"Charlie, please—"

"No!" I make the hex sign with my fingers. "The only thing

I want to hear out of your mouth is an apology for leaving me after my family died."

Just then, a loud thud hits the floor.

Julius fell off the bed in the midst of a seizure.

I sprint to his side. "No. No. No. No."

"What's wrong with him?"

"He has epilepsy. Can you please get me some water and a damp towel?"

He rushes to the bathroom and comes out a second later.

I dip Julius's paws in the water to keep him from overheating then place the damp towel on his head.

"Should I call the vet?" he asks.

I pet my dog's forehead, trying to comfort him. "We're used to this."

Eli kneels down next to me. "How can I help?"

A few seconds later, Julius's eyes roll back to normal and his body finally stops shaking. "There we go. All over." He buries his nose in my lap and pants.

Eli's hand travels to the small of my back.

I so want to lean on him and cry.

I struggle to lift my eighty-pound dog on the bed. "You can go now."

He takes him from me. "I got him. You still sleep on the right side?"

I close my eyes and nod.

Effortlessly, he places Julius on the left side and caresses his head. "Glad you're okay, pal."

This is too much for me. I press my palms over my eyes and bite down hard on my trembling lips.

All of a sudden, I'm in Elliott's arms. He's carrying me to bed.

I can't bear to look at him or thank him. Instead, I curl around Julius. The other dogs jump up and settle around me.

He chuckles. "Still sleeping in a pile of animals, I see."

These words are like an Exacto blade slicing open a decade-old scar. He knows me too well.

I can't take this anymore. It's one thing losing control of my body, but I can't lose control of my heart.

"It's been a long day," I say.

He nods. "Okay. Let me know if you need anything."

"I don't."

He heads for the door then halts. "I'm sorry," he says. "I never meant to hurt you."

Then he leaves. Again.

TWENTY-THREE

Eli Ties

Survival Tip*: Do not allow anyone to smoke if fuel has been spilled. Also, don't let intoxicated campers blunder off into unknown terrain.*

Eli's Mixtape: Beastie Boys, "Sabotage"

AT OUR PREGAME meeting the next morning, Skip asks us to name our team. "We need something to cheer from the sidelines."

"How about the Biggest Losers?" Avery suggests.

Skip gives her a down-the-nose stare. "I was thinking the Shimura Samurai."

"Sounds super lame," Sam says.

Skip jumps right over Sam's comment. "I did a little light reading last night." He flashes his phone. "Sun Tzu, *The Art of War*. Good stuff. Now that we're tied with Orion, I'd like to implement some of these strategies."

He pulls out a folded-up piece of notebook paper and sticks it to the bull's-eye on the dartboard.

Preeti rises from her chair and reads it aloud. "'Appear weak when you are strong, and strong when you are weak.'"

"Thank you, intern, you may be seated." He repeats the quote again. "As you know, we're the latter—"

Sabrina snorts. "We're a ladder?"

I press my palms together over my mouth. How did I end up in bed with her? Did we ever discuss anything besides body parts? Never mind, we all know the answer to that.

"Anywho…" Skip continues. "What I think old Sun meant is we need to up our trash talk game. During the snowmobile race, we shall cut down our opponents with our cutting wit." He slides a glance at Sabrina. "And you will concentrate on driving."

"What is trash talk?" Preeti asks.

Jerry puffs up his chest. "I'm a pro at 'dis."

Preeti takes out a small notebook and pen and jots down notes.

"First, you gotta insult somebody's ma. Then their bedroom skills. Dick size. Intelligence. Just keep going until they cry like a baby."

The intern scrawls notes on her pad. "So I should insult all of the family members or just the maternal figure?"

"Mostly the mom," Jerry says. "Here's an example." He turns to Skip. "Yo' mama's so fat, she uses epileptic boys as vibrators."

Skip pretends to blow chunks onto the floor.

"Ew, Jesus, Jerry," Avery says.

"Preeti," I shake my head. "Just…no."

Sam stretches and yawns. "I don't think we'll need to do much trash talking today. I've got a good feeling about today's race." The developer pulls a pocketknife out, opens it, and starts cleaning his fingernails with it.

Skip gives him a slanted side-eye. "What did you do, Fischer?"

A corner grin ticks. "Nothing, Samurai."

Avery collapses back on the floor. "I had exactly one hour of sleep last night because Austin was kicking me in the vagina. Now I have to race a snowmobile around a track when I've never even been on bumper car. Speak up, Sam, before I take that knife and cut out your heart. Do we have to race, or not?"

He winks. "I plead the fifth."

Avery shivers. "Is it weird that I'm turned on right now?"

"Is it weird I hired a serial killer?" Skip says.

This conversation is getting on my last nerve. So much so that the soothing belly breaths I'm pulling in are drawing looks from the intern.

I'm a wreck. My meditation this morning morphed into a heavy masturbation session in the shower.

"Also," Skip points out, "I think we need a team cheer. You know, like football teams? What rhymes with Shimura? Avery? You're the copywriter."

"Want to know what rhymes with Shimura? Let's get this goddamned thing over with," she says.

Jerry points out the obvious, as usual. "That doesn't rhyme."

"Amen," I say. "Let's go."

"All right, Samurai." Skip raises a fist. "Let's win this race."

Outside, Proton's owners await us on the field. Red flags mark a rough track that zigzags through the trees, around the lake, over another field, down a ravine, and back up again.

At the starting line, there are wooden stands. And on a log pole, they've installed speakers that are currently drilling feedback into my head.

Under the tent, near the starting line, Art, Burt, and Malcolm sit at the table and shoot the shit over the airwaves like professional sportscasters.

Art pants into the microphone like a sickening prank caller, and then chuckles and makes an announcement. "Here comes Shimura's team, looking pretty worn out after the Irish coffee this morning. Good luck guys. No drinking and snowmobiling. Heh, heh!"

Malcolm jumps in on the action. "Orion's team is dressed in Proton's latest winter line, looking fashionably sporty."

There are only eight snowmobiles total. So we have to choose two women and two men from each side. Through a very scientific game of eenie-meenie-miney-mo, Skip chooses Jerry, Preeti, Sabrina, and me to compete.

Across the field, Charlie tosses her pigtails, and in slow motion, she glides over the snow.

I groan. "My head's not really in the game, dude. Maybe you should take my place."

"My head's not even on this planet." Skip's eyes are just barely open. "I just smoked some insane Death Star Kush, and all I see are marshmallows. I'm counting on you, St. James." He claps my shoulder. "Go forth and weaken the enemy." His gaze goes skyward. "That's a weird word, enemy. Sounds like enema. Enemy. Enema. Enemy." He shakes his head and wanders away, repeating the words endlessly.

Malcolm presses the bullhorn button about twenty times.

Burt yanks the thing out of his hands and smacks him on the back. "Line up, gang."

Sam passes by me and mumbles, "Grab the four on the end before the other team does."

As if I needed any more stress. "You didn't do anything dangerous, did you? Like cut the brakes or some shit?"

"Nah. They're just newer models."

He's lying.

Art insists we go through this ridiculous shake-the-other-team's-hand thing.

Charlie takes off her glove before she reaches me and gives me a handshake that's more like foreplay. Her fingers trace my wrist and leave a lingering tingle.

My knees almost buckle.

"Ready to lose?"

An instant hard-on grows. No longer capable of rational thought, I brush my mouth against her ear. "If I win this race, I'm going to fuck you so hard tonight."

Hot surprise blooms on her cheeks, and then, *poof!* It's gone, and she morphs back into a surly kitty.

"And if I win," she purrs, "I'm going to grip that beard of yours in one hand and ride your face like a bronco."

I choke on my own saliva and pound my chest. Screw the Olympics. I've never wanted to win so bad in my life. I actually consider performing a series of light calisthenics to limber up. I also consider praying on my knees like Orion's receptionist.

Game on.

I swing my leg over the snowmobile and lower my goggles—ready to win, ready to ride, ready to get out of this cold and between her warm thighs. I rev the engine like it's a Harley. It sounds more like a lawnmower.

A flash goes off in my brain. It's as if I'm watching myself perform live onstage in a Seventies' sitcom. Where's the canned laughter? Where's the clapboard slamming shut? Where's the director shouting, "That's a wrap!"

Furthermore, where's my goddamn dignity?

"Hey, guy," Jerry says to Duffy. "You got sumptin' on your back." He flicks the copywriter's gray ponytail. "Oh, oops! Thought that was a rat."

Duffy doles out a tight smile. "Those 'roids affecting your vision, hoss?"

I tease Duffy. "Aw, did Jerry hurt your feewings?"

"Not as bad as I hurt his mom's last night when I told her to shave her face." Jerry slaps his thigh.

Christine gasps. "Jesus is watching."

"Is he watching this?" Sabrina flips her the bird.

I give her a soft fist bump. She is heretofore redeemed in my eyes.

She returns it with a look that says, "I've got your back, and I want you so bad."

Preeti reads a phrase out of her notebook to Charlie. "Your mother's breasts sag with such severity that the late, great surrealist artist, Salvador Dali, mistook them for clocks. Did I do that right, Jerry?"

He grins. "You did great, Preeti."

Charlie's farcical glower falters for a second.

That mom joke was just...*no*.

Preeti starts to fling another insult her way. "And your father has edema so terribly that—"

"All right, that's enough." I hush her up and direct my team to the vehicles Sam noted. "Are we gonna ride, or not?"

Malcolm shouts into the microphone. "Start your engines."

Art slaps his head with a glove. "They're already started."

Malcolm glares at his boss. "I'm suing for assault and battery."

"On your mark, get set...go!" Malcolm waves a flag like Rizzo in *Grease*, and we're off.

As we pass the stands, Skip raises a weak fist. "Go Samurai." Then he stumbles off the steps and lands on his ass in the snow.

Duffy's riding dirty, swerving in front of us, blocking our paths.

Sabrina gives him a flirty wave and blows a kiss.

He waves back, and she guns it past him.

Forget what I said, she's a genius.

And I'm right on her tail.

Charlie rides up on the bank, cranks a hard right, and crashes down in front of me.

I slam on my brakes. "I could have killed you!" While I'm trying to steady my trembling hands, she goes full-throttle and jets ahead.

Dammit!

Behind me, Jerry bellows to Duffy. "Get out of the way, old man!"

"Go fuck yourself, thug."

"Language," Christine yells.

Sabrina and Charlie are neck-and-neck in front. Stanley's just a hair behind them. I'm on his ass, and Duffy, Jerry, and Christine are trailing me. I glance over my shoulder. Preeti is nowhere in sight. Skip needs to fire her.

I grit my teeth. *Street rulz.* In pursuit of the two women who've driven me the craziest over the last few years, I blast through the trees and dart in front of them, laughing manically the whole time.

The race is five times around the track. We fly past the stands, completing the first lap.

"Nothing is happening," Malcolm says, sounding bored. "Oh my God, I just noticed Sabrina's coat. Love your coat, girl."

Avery and Austin cheer as we pass. Sam smirks. *Sneaky bastard.*

Jerry passes Duffy and Stanley, and Christine is on his ass. He's taunting her, slowing down, darting ahead, not letting her pass.

She lays on her horn. "You fucker!"

Jerry grabs the side of his face. "My virgin ears!"

Once again, I cackle like a madman then hug the curve like I'm on a motorcycle, and the snowy field is a high-tech speedway.

Head in the game, Eli, or you're not getting head.

On the fourth lap, Christine's snowmobile sputters and dies on the track. Jerry rams into the back of her and loses a front ski.

Preeti just barely misses them.

Sam. That sneaky bastard must have syphoned their gas.

Duffy and Stanley stall out a few lengths back.

I should feel guilty. But I don't.

Sabrina plows ahead and crosses the finish line first.

"Go Samurai!" I yell.

I'm so close to getting laid, so very, very, very, close.

Charlie's ride starts to slow.

I brake next to her and grin. "Problems?"

"Did you fuck with my gas tank?"

I cup my ear. "Sorry, didn't quite hear what you said. Did you ask me if I'm going to fuck you until you can't move later? Why, yes I am, Chicken."

We're moving at a snail's pace, and I'm deliriously happy, whistling Queen's "We Are The Champions."

Preeti shoots past us and crosses the finish line with her tongue out.

"Better hurry, Chicken." I sprint forward, slow down until she catches up, and then speed up again. "Can't wait to see your titties jiggling above my face." God, I love, love, love teasing her.

I'm so caught up in gloating and so lost in the imaginary hot porno of Charlie that I actually smile when she super-leaps over to my vehicle and shoves me off in one move.

Hopelessly ambushed, I roll off into the snow like a dead body thrown off a speeding train, and she roars across the finish line on my damn snowmobile.

It happened so quickly I didn't even have time to wipe the grin off my face.

I still have a hard-on!

No fear. None whatsoever. She's crazy.

Goddammit, she turns me on.

In spite of myself, I chuckle and brush the snow off my pants. I adopt a cool swagger as I cross the finish line, thumbs-upping my coworkers and grinning like an idiot.

She may have beaten me, but we still won. And I'm still going to stick my dick in her.

"Ladies and gentlemen," Burt announces, "we have a tie!"

I stop in my tracks. "What? What!" I march over to the judge's table, wild and rabid, like a methhead banned from buying cold medicine. "Tie? Tie! There was no tie! We won fair and square." I'm lying through my teeth, but that's beside the point.

Burt slaps his hands on the table and stares me down. "You got something to say, Bearded Clam?"

I slam my fist on the table. "This whole thing is rigged! Rigged, I tell you! Rigged!"

"The other snowmobiles have been tampered with," he says with his best Clint Eastwood impression. "Therefore, it's a tie."

We lock eyes and snort like bulls. Somewhere in the back of my mind, sane Eli taps my shoulder. *Um, what are you doing, yelling at an old man?*

I unfurl my fists and roll my shoulders.

Sabrina appears by my side. "This race is super illegitimate, guys."

Ever so calmly, I turn to her. "What the fuck are you talking about?"

"Duh. The race. It's not legit."

Two steps away, Charlie muffles a laugh into her scarf.

I storm off. "I need a drink." But first, I need to jack off.

Halfway back to the lodge, I halt in my tracks. *Wait a minute.* We tied. We fucking tied!

I raise my fists to the sky like I just won a gold medal. "Scoooooore!"

Game on, Chicken.

TWENTY-FOUR

Eli Plays Two Minutes In The Closet

ORION	SHIMURA
3	3

Survival Tip: *Sooner or later when traveling by compass, you will stray off course. When this happens, attempt a reverse azimuth to return to the last known point.*

Eli's Mixtape: Queens of the Stone Age, "The Way You Used To"

I STALK my prey during dinner. I watch her smell each bite of food before she eats it. I watch her twirl a lock of hair around her finger. I watch her sneak glances at me and touch her neck.

The flush in her cheeks is feverish, and wanton lust glistens in her gaze.

A flirty laugh floats out. It's like love birds singing.

Our brows lift in unison. Our lips part at the same time. Our chairs scrape the wood floor in concert.

We take our plates to the kitchen. Her dish clatters in the sink. Mine crashes on top of it.

I stand behind her, my breath blowing the silken threads of her hair. I scoop her ponytail out of the way and kiss the back of her shoulder.

Her neck stretches like a swan.

Then I grab her and yank her into the pantry, barring the door with a mop.

It's dark, and all I hear is panting. I feel around and pull the light cord.

"It's too bright," she says.

"The better for me to see you, my dear. Mwahahaha."

She swooshes her mouth to the side.

For a moment, we stand there, not moving.

She jams her hands on her hips. "Well?"

"Well, what?"

"You going to fuck me, or what?"

And we crash together, tearing at each other's zippers, ripping our shirts over our heads, gnashing our teeth together.

We do this five-second jack off—me making sure her pussy is swamped for me—it is—and her making sure I'm hard—I am and have been for an hour—then I grab her tit and bend her over.

I've got my dick lined up against her juicy opening, and panic slams into me.

"Oh, fuck."

"What?"

"I forgot a condom."

"I'm on the pill."

I give her a look.

One of her eyes squints like Forest Whitaker. "You're the only man I've ever slept with without one."

And I'm in. So in. So fucking in. I thrust hard and deep.

She mewls.

I give it to her again.

"God, you feel good," she says.

"You feel magical."

She leans back, and we kiss. Our tongues tangle in a dance of passion.

I straighten so I can watch myself burrow in and out of her, my dick shiny and wet. I split apart her cheeks and thumb her asshole, feeling the head of my cock through the layer of skin between us.

She rubs her clit.

I bring her pussy-soaked finger to my mouth and take over the duty. It's clean and salty. I want more.

I slide out and drop to my knees, eating her out from behind, tongue-fucking her hole.

Whimpers and vibrations and all the right signals sound out from above. "Hurry, get back inside me," she cries.

Perfect timing, because my cock feels dry and lonely. One more lick and I'm back in, pinning her arms against a wall of cereal boxes.

Squeeze, pluck, fuck, slam, suck. Squeeze, pluck, fuck, slam, suck. My rhythm now established, I hold her tight, her back pressed against my chest.

Her head rests on my shoulder, and her arms wind back around my neck.

We mash our mouths together.

"Mmmm," I moan.

In response, her pussy hugs my cock.

How I've missed your cunt, I want to say, but don't, because I've got a mouthful of her.

My skin slaps against hers, her ass shakes, I'm playing with her tits, and her hand is between us, rolling my balls.

My left fingers come into play—circling her hard clit, just barely touching it, the way she likes it.

"Elliott," she begs and slams her ass back against me.

I fold her over again and put my right hand to work—one finger in her tight asshole.

The shelf is wobbling, the floor is creaking, and she's chanting, "Fuck me. Fuck me."

I'm slamming inside her, come leaking from the tip of my cock, the scent of her arousal fueling me.

Her slippery flesh pulses and tightens around my cock.

The announcement arrives, the one I've been so eager to hear. "I'm coming!" she cries.

Her legs tremble, and her back arches, and I plunge deeper and rub faster and suck and bite her shoulder (the good one).

A sack of flour falls off the shelf and bursts open. White powder clouds around us.

At the base of my balls, a storm swirls, and I murmur dirty words. "I'm going to fuck this pussy raw." I crack my hand against her ass. "I'm going to fill it with cum."

She grinds hard against me. "I love your filthy mouth."

A jar of pickles rolls off the shelf and crashes to the floor right as I jet hot streams of cum inside her.

Her muscles clench and massage the last drop from my tip.

My ears ring. My heart pounds. I think I bit my tongue.

And then it's over.

I hunch over her back and suck her sweet, sweaty skin.

She lets out a puff of air, and her vagina releases a hot wash of cum down her thighs.

I smear it over her pussy lips, like I'm marking her with my brand.

Then we stand, turn around, and look at each other. We're covered in flour and sweat and cum. Our socks are sopping wet with pickle juice.

She cracks up.

I cover her mouth. "Shh! Someone will hear."

Her eyes roll.

I yank up my boxer shorts and glance around. "Jesus. We made a mess." I sniff the air. "It smells like pickled sex."

Silent laughter shakes her shoulders.

She grabs a dustpan, and I grab a mop. And like busy little beavers, we clean up our mess.

Then, as usual, our fun is interrupted by a goddamned knock on the door.

We freeze, our eyes bugged out.

"Helloooo," Malcolm sings on the other side. He taps again lightly. "When you kids are done banging in there, can you grab the broom and sweep up the kitchen? 'Kay, thanks. Bye."

We wait to speak until the clop of his clogs disappears.

"Think anyone else heard?" she asks.

"I don't care."

She worries her bottom lip.

"Do you?"

Her gaze lowers. "Alan."

"Alan," I repeat. Cold, hard steel—that's what my body turns into.

"It's complicated."

I knew it. I knew I should have steered clear of her. "Complicated as in, you're-still-fucking-your-employee complicated?"

Her head jerks up, and her brows stitch together.

For an agonizingly long time, I wait for her to clue me in. It never happens, which tells me they are a recently deceased couple, or worse, they're still screwing.

"Right," I say and fling open the door. "I'm out."

"Wait." She grabs my wrist. "Let me explain."

I shake her off and keep on walking. Too late. I'm already done.

I fucking hate games.

TWENTY-FIVE

Charlie Makes Love

March 2003

My roommate and I concocted a brilliant plan. I'm going to tell Elliott I lost my cherry to some fictitious guy.

If all goes as planned, he'll be begging me for booty by the end of the week.

TWENTY-SIX

Charlie Gets Zapped

Eli's Mixtape: BROS, "Tell Me"

THE STRONG SCENT of static electricity surrounds me in the night. A heavy cloud cover insulates the mountain, making the temperature unseasonably warm. Lightning flashes over the nearby peaks, and thunder rumbles in the distance.

I take this rare winter thunderstorm as a message from the universe—lightning never strikes the same place twice. I don't know if we can do this again. I don't know if we'll ever be able to move on.

My face burns from his whiskers. Between my legs, I'm raw and freshly fucked. I close my eyes and replay the scene in the pantry. His hands on me. The feel of him inside me. His strength. His need. His cum, drying in my panties.

The pickles.

His angry departure.

I shouldn't have let him go.

At the time, a voice inside me said, *don't chase after him. If he doesn't want an explanation, don't give it to him. If he's not going to stick around, then let him go.*

I wish I could let him go.

It's like I've got one hand desperately clinging to a cliff, trying not to fall. What's at the bottom? What happens when the last thread connecting me to my childhood disappears? Do I disappear?

Who am I, anyway? And why am I outside in a lightning storm talking to myself at 1:00 a.m.? I need answers.

I need help.

Had Elliott chosen to stay instead of leave, I would have explained why the Alan situation is so complicated.

For one thing, Alan handles the company's operations. He has access to all of my bank accounts. He has my passwords and controls all of the money. He has copies of my keys. He pays the bills and the payroll. He's the one who set up Orion's firewall. He handles the taxes and client invoicing.

My business is utterly dependent on him. If I destroy Alan's trust, he could destroy the only thing I have left in this world—my business.

Also, he's extremely sue-happy. Together with my legal team, he's fought and won dozens of patent suits, copyright theft issues, branding problems, personnel issues—the list goes on.

When I refuse to fight, he lights the torch and chases after the monsters for me.

And sleeping with him then firing him a short while later is serious grounds for a lawsuit.

I have no access to a computer here. I'm in the middle of a pitch. I can't just drop everything and change my bank accounts. Giving him the heave-ho will take serious preparation.

What was I thinking, giving a man such control over my life?

The thing is I'm not even sure I have to fire him. Maybe he'll get the hint soon or find someone else to obsess over.

For now, I have to put up with his constant personal space invasions. Besides, it's not like I'm leading him on. I'm just not turning him off.

If Elliott can't stop running away every time a fire breaks

out, then I'm not going to put my business in jeopardy by dealing with Alan before I'm ready.

If he can't handle the Chicken, he needs to get the hell out of the kitchen.

Who needs him, anyway?

Who needs my old best friend, the love of my life, the best sex I've ever had, and the only man who's met the real me?

For an instant, back in the closet, for one single solitary second, I felt fulfilled. I thought when it was over, I wouldn't be alone anymore, and that finally, *finally*, I had someone to share my life with.

I'm always wrong.

The wind kicks up and drops of sleet prick my face. The pain feels good. It's a subtle reminder I'm still alive.

Drenched and frozen, I hurry back to the lodge, wondering how this bizarre weather will affect tomorrow's activities.

Over dinner, my godparents announced we'd be building cardboard bobsleds and racing them in the afternoon.

I'm not sure I can handle another day of these crazy games. I know I can't handle another day trapped next to Elliott.

Please, Mother Nature, shut it all down! Cancel work tomorrow. I need a day off. I need a sick day.

TWENTY-SEVEN

Eli Rides A Chicken

Survival Tip: *Mouth-to-mouth resuscitation, or "the kiss of life," is fast and effective. Begin as soon as the airway has been cleared. Normal recovery is rapid, except in cases of shock.*

Eli's Mixtape: Vanilla Ice, "Ice Ice Baby"

It's like the White Witch enslaved Breckenridge in an eternal winter.

A freak ice storm hit last night and imprisoned everything in frozen glass.

This kind of weather hits the Northeast all the time, but here in Colorado it never happens.

Climate change—a reminder that humanity can and will be crushed for its crimes against nature.

It's shockingly beautiful, the bright sun reflecting off the crystalline surface. Icicles drip off the tree branches like Christmas ornaments.

The ground is a sparkly slick dance floor. I'm serious. It's impossible to walk on that stuff. You need crampons to get around.

The electricity shut off last night, and we woke up this morning seeing our own breath. Luckily, the lodge has a backup generator, but it only provides enough power for two rooms. So the Orion team is in the living room, and we're clustered in the game room, building our stupid bobsleds.

Malcolm, dressed in a Snuggie, arrives and plops a pile of cardboard and a bag of supplies on the floor. "Have at it," he says.

Avery pulls a pink box from the sack. "What's this?"

"Feathers."

"You expect us to build a sled out of feathers?" She lifts another item out of the bag. "And a Bedazzler?"

He gives her a melodramatic shrug. "Like I told Art, it's not wise to let a gay man loose in a craft store. I can't be held responsible for my decisions. Not with all of those rhinestones and tubes of puffy paint and fifty thousand bottles of glitter. It's like dangling a bottle of Mad Dog in front of a wino and expecting him to walk on by."

"What'd you give the other team?" I ask.

"I don't know, but I got a sweet Dolly Parton paint-by-number kit on clearance." He slides me a side glance. "My room is next to the kitchen if you want to come check it out."

"No, thanks," I tell him.

"Meh, thought I'd ask." Then he sashays out of the room with his Snuggie trailing behind him.

Skip presses his palms to his eyes. "Is this really my life now? Crafting?"

Preeti tries to cheer him up. "We're tied with Orion. We can still win this."

That gives him a slight boost. He slides out of his chair and crawls over to the pile of supplies. "Well, at least we have duct tape."

With Charlie's vagina no longer a trophy, my enthusiasm is at an all-time low, and it was never that high to begin with.

Building this stupid bobsled has really put my compassion to test. I'm tired of my coworkers. Every single one of them.

But at least they agree to build my sled design. Mostly because they don't care.

I can't wait to see Charlie's face when she sees this thing.

Once the glitter and puffy paint dries, we trek out to the "sled run" behind the lodge. In reality, it's not so much of a sled run as it is a ninety-degree death drop.

But who cares if we die? As long as I get to witness Alan slip and fall on his ass a few more times, I'm good with it.

Charlie's expression when she sees our giant cardboard chicken also makes our imminent demise worthwhile.

I wish I could have captured it on film. That, and the adorable Sullivan pathetic-excuse-for-a-surly-scowl that followed.

To go with her adorable glare, she's wearing one of those sheepskin hats with the flaps over the ears turned up like a puppy. Her hair is tied in messy pigtails like when she was a little girl.

I also wish I would have been able to control my sprawling smile. It made it seem like I'm not mad at her. And trust me, I'm mad. Mad enough to go balls out in a bobsled race.

Jerry and Preeti dole out an adequate amount of trash talking. We all make fun of Orion's dumb Dead Mobile, which was clearly Duffy's suggestion.

Shimura's game plan for this race is more or less organized chaos. No one's in charge. It's a free for all.

Charlie's phony laughter is turned on full blast today. Like a hummingbird, she flies around her staff, chirping brightly, laughing artificially—spreading sweet nectar, boosting their spirits.

What must it be like to work with her?

It's like scaling a glacier to get to the top of the run. Proton should have made that the competition.

Each sled seats four. Sabrina and Avery ride in the middle of ours. I'm steering the ship and Skip's in the back.

The rest of our crew is responsible for the push off. Not that we need one on this killer ice. What we really need is brakes. Also, we used a pound of snowboard wax on the bottom. That was before we saw the run.

I pull on the rope and test the wings on the side. The left doesn't move.

"Uh, oh," Sabrina says. "The glue must have frozen."

Avery shakes her head. "If I die, will one of you take care of my kid?"

Fischer volunteers. "I'll do it. I love your kid."

"Someone other than Sam?"

He actually looks hurt.

There's a minor scuffle on the other team, and Duffy moves to the back, letting Charlie drive. She slides her goggles over her hat and throws the end of her red scarf over one shoulder. She looks like Snoopy about to fight the Red Baron.

I swallow a chuckle.

Chin lifted and mouth straight, she gives me a curt nod then hunches over her sled's reins.

A rush of adrenaline pumps through me and renders me stupid. I'm still gawking at her when Malcolm waves the flag at the bottom of the hill.

Suddenly, we're dashing down the run like a jet ready for takeoff.

Sabrina's arms circle my waist so tightly I can barely breathe. The sharp wind dries out my eyes and mouth, which is currently in a wide-open Jack-o'-lantern grin.

"They're gaining on us, dude," Skip cries.

That's absolutely ludicrous since we're moving at a clip of at least fifty miles an hour. We're on a freaking luge.

"What do you want me to do?" I shout back.

"The wings have got to go." He rips one off and tosses it in Orion's path.

They veer into us to avoid it. I rock to the side, desperately trying to avoid a collision.

A woman screams. Or was that Skip? "Watch out!"

I didn't even see what we hit. Later they told me it was a fallen tree trunk buried under the snow.

The impact tears the bottom out of our sled and my teammates are left in a puff of pink feathers and glitter.

Meanwhile, I fly over the bump, still clinging to the chicken head, and zoom down the mountain, headed straight for Burt and Art.

Just before I wipe them out, I let go and do a stunt roll.

Charlie whizzes past me, sans bobsled, spread-eagle on her stomach, her puffy jacket and snow pants providing zero traction.

Wildly out of control and laughing like a lunatic, she keeps going and going and going, past the finish line, all the way to the middle of the frozen lake and then stops with a tiny grunt.

Her dogs fly past us, the three-legged one moving the fastest, and I'm right behind them, the icy snow under my feet shattering like glass.

The Saint Bernard reaches her first. He grabs her scarf in his mouth and tries to drag her off the ice to safety.

What he's really doing is strangling her.

Every curse word I've ever known flies out of my mouth. Swearing is the only thing I can do at this point, to keep her dog from killing her.

Ten feet from her, my feet slide out from under me and I crash down on my bad knee. I fall so hard it rattles my teeth, and I almost black out.

Wincing in pain and gripping my knee, I crawl to her dog and try to tear the scarf from his jowls.

He thinks it's a game and keeps tugging.

Legs kicking and flailing, Charlie tears at her neck, her eyes bugged out and face turning blue.

"Goddammit, let go!" I grab the dog's tail and yank so hard he yelps and drops the scarf.

She gasps and wheezes and chokes, tears streaming down her face.

Still cringing in pain, I slide over to her, unravel her scarf and start performing CPR.

Her tongue darts up and swirls around mine.

I jerk back and smile. "You're alive!"

She smacks my chest and shoves me. "Get off me, you big lug."

"You could have died, if it weren't for me."

Her smile melts. She doesn't thank me. In fact, she almost looks disappointed.

She calls for her killer mutt. "Come here, L.L."

The dog crawls over to her, his expression full of guilt.

She kisses his head. "It's okay. I'm fine. I know you were just trying to help." From her pocket, she pulls out a strip of bacon and gives it to him.

He's all licks and wagging tails after that.

Where's *my* bacon? My knee throbs to the same beat as my pulse.

"Hey, Bearded Clam," Burt yells from shore. "My goddaughter okay?"

I don't answer him. Instead, I shoot a vicious glare at her. "Goddaughter?"

Her brows knit together. "You didn't know that?"

Rapid-fire breaths shoot out of my nostrils. "No wonder!"

"He was at the funeral." Her voice is scratchy and strained.

A wave of nausea rolls over me. The only thing I remember from that horrible day is Charlie's blank face and her hand holding mine so tightly my fingers went numb.

It all makes sense now. That's why the old bastard has been giving me grief. "Does he know about us?"

"I don't think he remembers."

"Yeah, I bet. So this whole thing's just a big joke? Just a rich man's idea of revenge? Is that why I'm here?"

"No!" She seems to mull it over for a minute. "I don't think so. He wouldn't do that. I'm pretty sure he doesn't know who you are."

I try to stand, but my injured knee buckles, and I land back on my ass.

"Did you hurt yourself? Is that your bad knee? Think you can walk? Hold on. Let me help you." She stumbles to her feet and holds out her hands.

Refusing to look weak and helpless, I don't take them.

"Elliott."

"I'm good."

"No, you're not."

I ignore her and bend my knee. It's on fire.

"You stubborn ass!"

All right, that's it. I've had it. "Me? Me! I'm the stubborn ass? You've got some nerve, lady."

She smirks. "Lady?"

"You're enjoying this, aren't you? Me in pain. You probably planned this whole thing." I pop my jaw and mumble. "Sadist."

"What did you say?" Her words come out in little stabs.

"You heard me. It brings you pleasure, hurting me, doesn't it? Bet you loved telling me about your little boyfriend after I fucked you in the closet." I scoff again. "Do you get off on this? Does he know? Is he in on the game? Is everyone out to mind fuck me?"

A crowd of our coworkers gather at the lake's edge. *Great*, now we have an audience.

"He is not my boyfriend! I don't want him! What does it matter? It's over! You left!"

She's not referencing my departure from the closet. She's talking about ten years ago.

I lower my voice. "I didn't leave you. I took some time to think."

Her gaze smacks me hard. "You didn't tell me where you went or when you'd be back. You just left."

Then I see it, the almost imperceptible tremble of her bottom lip, the tiny clue that she's hurting too. This isn't fun for her. It's causing her as much agony as it is me.

As if we're standing in the eye of a hurricane, everything stills. And in that moment, it occurs to me—I've never seen her break down. Not even at the funeral. Not when I walked out the door. Not when her boyfriend dumped her in high school, and I took his place at the prom. Not when the jealous girls in her class shunned her for being a tomboy. She probably doesn't even know how to cry.

I struggle to my feet and stand in front of her, studying the hidden fragility behind those gold flecks. "I didn't leave you, Charlie," I say softly.

She turns her back to me and lowers her head.

The desperate need to comfort her claws at me. I tug her pigtail gently. "Charlie. Look at me."

She doesn't move.

"I didn't leave you." What I did was much, much worse.

"You idiots gonna stand out there all day?" Burt hollers. "You realize you're on a lake? I'm not fishing your asses out of the ice, if you fall through."

I wave him off. Another slice of silence passes between us. "Look, we can't change the past. But maybe we can…"

She wipes her eyes and faces me. "What?"

"Maybe we can, I don't know, just be…"

"Be what?"

"That's it. Just be." I can't even believe I made such a Zen statement, particularly since my mind is nowhere near Zenlandia at the moment. "Let's not look back or forward. Let's just stay right here."

She sniffles. "On the lake?"

"I'm speaking metaphorically, asshole."

A grin cracks, and it's like the sun has broken through the clouds. "I know, dickhead. I'm just trying to bring a little levity to the situation."

We stand there for a minute longer, reflecting each other's sad smiles.

"Here, lean on me." She offers her bum shoulder.

I shake my head and sigh. "Aren't you ever going to get tired of this? The invincible act?" I tip her chin up. "Hmm? What's it going to take for you to finally admit you're the one who needs help?"

As usual, she evades the question, and we hobble across the ice. When we reach the dock, I help her up and she helps me up.

Then she puts her hands on her hips and squints one hilarious evil eye. "I won, you know."

"No, you didn't."

"Yes, I did."

"You didn't, but I'm sure your *godfather* will award you the point regardless. Wait until Skip finds out you're related to him."

Her arm holds me back. "Please, don't tell him."

"Not cool."

She rolls her lip under her teeth as if contemplating the next words carefully. "I'm not ready. For you to leave. Not yet."

Me, neither. But I'm not willing to admit that out loud. Just like all the other things I'm not going to confess.

TWENTY-EIGHT

Eli Loses A Mom

Survival Tip: Children need reassuring and comforting, especially if they are lost or in pain.

Eli's Mixtape: Jack Johnson, "Love Song #16"

LATER THAT AFTERNOON, the power comes back on in the lodge. Charlie disappears, along with everyone else, presumably to take a nap.

Taking advantage of her absence, I kick back and read a book in the living room while Burt, Art, and Sam watch the Broncos play.

Malcolm shuffles out in a smoking jacket and leopard print boxer briefs. There's a tissue stuffed up each nostril. He puffs out a coy cough. "I've got the consumption." He waves a tissue in front of his face like a handkerchief and coughs again. "I'm afraid I can't be your slave today."

Burt studies his employee. "You been taking acting lessons?"

Malcolm rolls his eyes. "Fine. I have a date with a ski bum named Phil. And if you don't let me go, I'll die right here."

Art snorts. "Where's Avery's kid?"

"The intern has him."

Preeti walks out holding Austin's hand. "It's fine. I'll watch him while his mom sleeps."

"You best be back to make breakfast. I'm not paying you an outrageous salary, with benefits and health club membership, so you can find the love of your life."

Malcolm waves a finger. "Let's not go there. This is more like a booty call."

"Get out of here before I change my mind."

At some point, everything goes fuzzy, and I fall asleep. An hour later, I wake up to the sound of Avery's voice.

"Has anyone seen Austin?"

I open one eye. Preeti's conked out on the other side of the sofa.

I sit up and scratch my head. "He was here just a second ago."

"Who?"

"Your kid. Preeti was playing with him. He can't be far."

Avery's nostrils flare slightly. She is not happy. For the next twenty minutes, she tears through the lodge, waking up everyone.

When she doesn't find him, her panic-mode turns on full blast. "He's nowhere. He's gone." She yanks on her coat. I do the same. So does Sam, Skip, and the rest of our team. Preeti tries to go with us.

"No!" Avery snaps. "You stay here. In case he comes back."

Burt and Art take off on the snowmobiles to case the area. Half of us search the perimeter of the house—the hot tub, the barn, and the garage.

The rest of us follow Avery to the lake, stumbling and tripping on the snow, still slick with ice.

We circle the rim, examining the ice for cracks where he might have fallen in.

"He's not here, Ave," Sam says in a soothing voice. "The only footprints here are from adults."

That causes Avery to explode. "Then where *is* he?"

Sam grips her shoulders. "Honey, you're hyperventilating. Take a breath, please."

She finally breaks down. "If I lose him, I'll die. He's all I have."

Sam pulls her in for a hug.

"We'll find him, Ave," I tell her. "He can't be far. He's probably hiding." I run back to the house and check every nook and cranny where a kid could possibly hide.

I bolt upstairs and pass by Charlie's room. Her door is cracked, and the dogs are at the foot of the bed. I can't see them, but I hear their whispers.

Relief washes over me. She found him.

Her red boots stick out from the end of the bed. While she whispers to Austin, her toes click together.

I eavesdrop for a moment.

"I don't have a daddy either," she says.

"Why not? Did a monster eat him?" he asks. "That's what happened to mine."

"A monster ate your dad?"

"Yeah, a purple one."

"That's scary. Is that why you're hiding?"

"No, I'm playing hide and seek."

"Your mommy is very worried," she says.

"Why?"

"She thinks something bad happened."

"Like a monster ate me?"

"Exactly. So you've got to come out of there, before she calls the police."

"I don't wanna."

I crouch down and lift the covers. "Hey, little man. What are you doing under there?" I can't see him.

Charlie points to a tear in the box spring cover. That's why we didn't see him before. He's concealed under the black fabric.

"I'm hiding," he whispers.

"But how will Santa find you when he comes to leave the presents?" I ask.

That does the trick. The fabric rips, and the toddler tumbles out on top of Charlie. "Ow! That hurt. Uh-oh. Elliott? We're stuck."

I lift the mattress, and they crawl out. "How'd you find him?"

"The dogs kept messing around under my bed," she says.

"Pretty good hiding place, little man." I lift him over my shoulders, and the kid grabs my hair like reins. "Boy, your mom's going to be super happy to see you."

"Giddyap!" Austin cries.

I neigh like a horse.

Charlie flashes me a sparkly smile that warms my center.

"What?" I ask.

She shakes her head. "You're awfully cute, stallion."

"You hear that, dude?"

"Boys aren't cute," Austin says.

"Darn right. Let's go find your mom." I whinny and gallop down the stairs.

The reunion is like something out of a *Lifetime* movie. Avery, blotchy faced and half-crazed, sobs and squeezes her kid. "I'm so happy to see you." Then she spanks his butt hard.

Austin wails.

"You are in big trouble, little boy." She raises her hand again.

Sam grabs her by the wrist. "Okay, he got the point."

"I'm going to kill him. Swear to God."

Sam chuckles and hauls her up. "How about we take a family dip in the hot tub and relax for a bit?"

Avery drenches Sam's shirt with tears.

She's not the only one crying. Preeti is also flipping out. She's in Skip's arms, and he's practically cooing in her ear.

"It's not your fault," he tells her. "He's just being a kid. She's not mad at you."

"Yes, I am!" Avery shouts.

Sam steers her out of the room. "Okay, get your swimsuit on."

I feel the Sullivan burn on the back of my neck. I glance over my shoulder and eye the culprit up and down. "Are you checking out my ass?"

"Maybe," Charlie says, then slinks away like an angry kitty, swishing her tail.

I want to chase after her. But I don't. I've chased after her for far too long.

TWENTY-NINE

Eli Goes Hunting

Survival Tip: To attract a rescue party, start a fire and place it in a triangle.

Eli's Mixtape: The Black Keys, "The Girl Is On My Mind"

PROTON DROPS us off in Breckenridge the next evening for a scavenger hunt. This time, Art splits us into guys and girls teams. Which means I'm working with that tool, Alan, along with the other guys on Orion's team.

The town, with its old street lanterns, holiday lights, and quaint buildings, looks like a Hollywood set for a Christmas movie.

Clydesdales clomp down the street, dragging red sleighs behind them. Vendors sell hot chocolate and roasted cinnamon nuts in sidewalk huts.

It's adorable. And for a moment, I think about what it would be like to live here. I could teach snowboard lessons during the winter and be a backpacking guide in the summer.

Then Jerry Reno's honking laughter wipes out my daydream, and I turn back to the insidious task of searching for dumb stuff.

The list Art's given us is on par with something a church group would do. *Find a postcard of the ski area. Buy a bag of roasted chestnuts.*

Skip reads off the list then crumples the paper and chucks it in the trash. "Screw that. Let's go get a drink."

"I'm so down for that," Wang says.

There is heartfelt agreement on both sides.

And so we wander down to a bar on the corner and get seated at a table for eight. After the second pitcher of beer, Jerry starts telling raunchy jokes. The socially awkward forced laughter from the other team keeps him going until Skip shuts him up.

By the third pitcher, the topic switches to women. Stanley talks about his ex-wife. Duffy talks about his marriage. Wang hints at his relationship with Joy.

Skip flies up and sits at the bar. He's done.

So am I.

I wander over and sit next to him. He's flipping through his phone furiously, tapping his finger loudly against the screen.

"Everything okay, man?" I ask.

He sets down his phone and stares at his beer. "Not really."

"You worried about the games?"

"I'm going to have to lay off people at the beginning of the year."

I don't say anything. Because what can you say?

"Callie Murphy just texted me. She wants me to be her bridesmaid. She and her sister are getting married on Valentine's Day."

Callie is Skip's good friend. She and her fiancé, Walker, used to work at the agency until they went on a cross-country blog tour for our RV client.

Recently, she published a book, and Walker became a big shot photographer. Now they live in Georgia somewhere.

"No shit? I thought they were already married." I stop and think. "Wait a minute. Elias and Effie are getting married, too? That *puto* never called me. Then again, I don't have a phone."

Skip's vacant expression stays put.

"Are you upset she asked you to be a bridesmaid?"

He sighs. "I just never thought they'd go through with it."

"She's pregnant, right?"

"Yeah."

I get the feeling something went down between him and Callie. But I don't pry. Because that's not what men do. Instead, I ask him about something else that's been on my mind. "So what's your beef with Jerry? I get that he's kind of annoying, but he seems pretty harmless."

Skip pounds the rest of his beer. "Can you keep this locked inside the vault, St. James?"

I nod.

"Reno knew about the embezzlement and never told my father. He knew it was happening and just sat on his fat ass and didn't do anything."

Before Skip took over the agency from his father, some guys at the top ran out of town with the agency's profits. The authorities still haven't found them, and it had a serious impact on the business. Something like a hundred people were laid off. I was one of the lucky ones.

Skip's been scrounging for work for the last couple of years, just barely keeping us afloat. Not many people know about this, but since I'm pretty tight with his friend, Callie, she filled me in.

"You serious?" I ask. "Why didn't you fire him?"

"Because I'm a nice guy. And because he begged me. He's got a disabled sister he's supporting."

"Still…"

He slides a glance Jerry's way. "I sincerely loathe that guy. The minute I win a new client, he's out."

"Why don't you do it now? Hell, I would."

"He's the only one who's got a grasp on the billing. Besides, I can't fire him during the holidays. I'm just not that kind of Grinch."

I study my boss for a moment. He pretends to be a clueless pothead who doesn't care about anyone. But really? He's one of the most compassionate dudes I know.

"Shots on me. What's your poison?"

"Tequila," he says.

I signal the bartender, and we down the liquor in one gulp.

Later, Sam ambles over and sits next to us. He swivels his stool toward me. "Listen, St. James, I'm not normally a pot-stirrer, but that Alan guy is talking shit about your woman."

I spin around and train my ears on the conversation.

"Oh yeah, she's been on my ass for years," Alan brags. "But I didn't want to mix business with pleasure." He folds his hands behind his head and cracks a dickish smile. "Should have taken her up on it before last month. Never knew she was a screamer."

I leap out of my seat, fists clenched and ready to take him out.

Sam blocks me with his arm. "He's not worth it. Come on. Let's take a walk."

"Go with him, St. James," Skip adds. "I can't afford to bail your ass out of jail."

On the way outside, I keep an I'm-going-to-fuck-you-up glare bolted to Alan. Then I storm down the sidewalk like a wild bull on the loose.

Sam keeps up with me, not saying a word.

Two blocks later, we halt at a dead-end street.

Sam rubs his arms and bounces up and down. "Shit, it's freezing out here. Should have grabbed our jackets."

I don't feel a thing. My rage is keeping me warm.

"That guy's lying," Sam says.

"What do you mean?"

"Special Ops. We're trained to read people. He's got a tell.

Rubs his nose. Nasal membranes flare up when you lie."

My anger blows out with a loud breath.

"So what's up with you and that chick?" he asks.

"We dated in college."

"Ah, you've got a history."

"It's complicated."

"Women are complicated."

"Amen."

"You cooled down, yet? My balls are about to break off."

We walk back in silence. At the bar door, Sam says, "I'm guessing that guy is packing a two-inch dick. Don't worry about that asshole. Your woman's got it bad for you."

"How do you know?"

"Told you, I can read people."

And just like that, I fall into bro-love with my sneaky coworker.

Inside, the women's team is at the table. The ambience has grown louder and more drunken.

I pull up a chair across from Charlie.

She gives me a shifty kitty glance.

A drum beats in my chest. I need to find out the truth. "Are you with Alan?"

Her answer is quick. "No."

"Do you want to be with me?"

"Yes."

I smirk, grab my coat, and nod to the door.

Her lips part, and she nods back. Signal received, loud and clear.

Outside, I dial an Uber. One is just around the corner. I stand in the cold, watching the ringlets of my breath.

Charlie's still at the table. Maybe she didn't get the signal after all.

The Uber dot comes closer.

She's not moving.

The car pulls up to the curb.

Just as I open the door, she bursts out of the bar and climbs in the back seat.

I let out an internal sigh of relief.

On the short trip back to the lodge, we say nothing. There's a foot gap between us.

She stays on her side.

I stay on mine.

When we arrive, I pay the guy, and Charlie tugs me around to the back of the lodge. We slip inside the back door and hurry up to her room. Even her dogs don't notice we're back.

I unzip my coat. She unzips hers. We take off our boots.

Electricity whizzes between us.

I make the first move and trace her bottom lip with my thumb.

She kisses it then sucks it.

I lift her sweater over her head and unsnap her bra.

She unbuttons my flannel and unzips my pants.

We're naked.

I'm hard.

She's wet.

But our gazes stay melded.

I lift her up, and she wraps her legs around my waist.

Her hand caresses my face, and finally, our mouths meet.

The kiss is sensual, delicious.

I set her down on the bed and crawl between her thighs, slowly, carefully, ready to take possession, but not wanting to rush it.

My cock presses against her heat, and I slide it up and down her slick layers, teasing her, glazing myself with her wetness.

She's trembling.

I'm throbbing.

Her tongue circles my nipple.

I play with hers, pinching them into hard peaks and pulling on them the way she likes.

Her hips grind against mine. She wants me inside.

A drop of pre-cum erupts from the tip of my prick.

She smears it over my cock then grips me tight.

I thrust inside her all the way to the hilt, and when I bottom out, she arches into me, her head tipping back and her eyelids closing halfway.

I hover my mouth just above hers—still keeping our hot gazes connected—and I roll my hips slowly, savoring the glorious squeeze of her cunt.

Then her eyes turn glassy, and her chin quivers.

What I'm doing to her pussy is so amazing it's actually brought tears to her eyes. I'm a master at turning her on.

Then, *wham!* All of a sudden, she shoves me, and my dick is out.

"What the hell!"

"You're making love to me."

"You just now figure that out?"

"You don't get to make love to me. You haven't earned that right."

I drag my hand down my face, wiping off my confused state. It smells like her. I glance at her glistening pussy, trying to make sense of this precarious situation. How do I get back inside there?

I pump my cock, because it feels good, and her lemon-pucker glare feels bad.

"Uh…" That's the most speech I can manage.

"You can fuck me. But that's it."

I clasp my hands in prayer. "Chicken, for the love of God, please tell me, what the fuck is the difference?"

Her chin lifts, and a tiny "hmpf" comes out.

I grunt. "Okay, okay, okay, okay, okay." I take a deep breath and continue. "How do I earn a pass?"

"Well," she says snootily. "You can start by rubbing your beard on my vagina."

I'm so confused. "So this is about foreplay?"

"No, this is about the slow, I-love-you sex and the steamy St.

James smirk."

You know what? I need to shut her up. So I grab her knees and yank her down to the edge of the bed.

❄

Eli's Mixtape: Missy Elliott, "Hot Boyz"

THE HEAT between her legs draws me in. I nuzzle, lick, and nibble my way toward the prize.

She tenses and pants as I peel her open and tongue-tease her smooth layers.

Her scent has always driven me wild. And her taste…

The grip she has on my hair is downright painful, but I stay focused on making her gyrate her pussy against my beard.

"Oh," she moans. "That feels so, oh, so rough, and, ooooh, don't stop, fun."

I twirl a finger inside her and press it against the back of her clit.

Her thighs lock around my ears.

I push her knees down and glance up for a second. My heart skips a beat.

This beautiful creature—so fierce and so reckless—is just about ready to break. And I'm going to shatter her to pieces.

I get more aggressive and faster. I suck her clit, pinch her lips, and flick her spot. My tongue has gone numb. My neck kind of hurts. But I want her to come so goddamn bad. I grip my cock and jerk it to the rhythm.

"What are you doing down there?" She lifts her head to check. "Oh, God. That's so hot. Keep going." Her legs tremble, and her head falls back.

Any minute now.

Whimpers build in frequency, and her squirms intensify. Then her thighs slam against my cheeks, and it's quiet, except for the ringing in my ears.

Her orgasm is silent, and by the looks of it, so very intense.
Dazed, I watch and pump my cock.
Her hips lower. She's panting, looking astonished.
"How was that?"
"Fucking great."
"My turn." I grab her waist and flip her over on her stomach so she's leaning over the bed. Once I'm back in, I yell out. "Sweet relief!"
This time I don't fuck around. My mission is to come as fast as possible.
The bed bangs against the wall while I bang her.
She slams her ass back into me, mewling and moaning.
Fast. Furious. Fucking.
The world goes white, and then… "Oooooh, yeah." In the distance, I hear my own voice. It sounds like a late-night DJ.
The millennium ends during that moment. And then…
"Are you okay?" She peers over her shoulder. "You're not moving."
"Can't."
She releases her hold on me, and I spill out of her.
"Stop." I gently push her over and spread her ass cheeks. As my cum pours out, my grin builds. "So beautiful."
She spins around and kisses me hard. Then she slaps me on the ass and sprints to the bathroom. "Let's take a shower."
While we bathe, I sing, I soap up, I bounce her tits in my hands. I suck her neck. I sing some more. I play with her pussy.
She plays with my cock.
We wash each other.
I suck her nipples.
She tugs my balls.
It's heavenly.
She giggles. "You're like a big puppy, splashing around in here."
"That doesn't sound very manly."
"Are you honestly questioning your manhood, after that

orgasm you gave me?"

Ready to give her another one, I shut off the tap and dry off like *The Flash*.

Just as fast, I whip back the bed covers, climb in, and pat the mattress.

She shakes a finger at me. "Oh no! You are not spending the night."

"Huh?"

"Get up. We are not lovers. We're not even friends. You haven't earned it."

"Huh?" I say again.

"Out!"

My sexual stupor dissolves. I haul my ass out of bed and tuck my clothes under an arm. "Woman, you drive me crazy. No lie. By the time this is over, I'm going to be a blubbering, drooling mess."

"Maybe you should meditate about it. Figure out why I'm kicking you out."

"Maybe I will," I say like a fourth grade boy.

"Hmpf!"

"Hmpf!"

I turn the handle.

"Oh, by the way," she says defiantly. "I won the hunt tonight."

"Goodie for you." I swing open the door.

"Lock it on the way out."

"You got it!" I slam it behind me. Her dogs bark and run upstairs.

Burt's on their tail with a loaded gun, cocked and ready to fire. "Who's there?" He spots me, naked and shivering in the shadows, then lowers his weapon. "Well, well. Look who's doing the walk of shame." He clucks his tongue and tromps back down the stairs, yucking it up the entire way down.

"Goodnight, Chicken," I shout.

"Goodnight, Loser!"

THIRTY

Charlie Doesn't Celebrate

December 2004

WEINER and I had a long conversation about Loser. He thinks the reason Elliott hasn't told anyone about us is because he's scared he's going to lose me.

That's all fine and dandy, but I'm tired of pretending I don't have a boyfriend. I'd seriously consider something *Fatal Attraction*-ish, but today he poured fifty pounds of sand in my apartment and rented a bunch of heat lamps. Since I can't leave because of finals, he said he was taking me on a beach vacation for Christmas.

I love that Loser.

Also, he cleaned everything up. That man makes me swoon. Don't tell him that.

THIRTY-ONE

Charlie's Got Talent

Eli's Mixtape: Phil Collins, "In The Air Tonight - 2015 Remastered"

ART RIDICULES US. "Pshaw! Everyone's got talent. *America's Got Talent.*" He's a little too amused with himself.

Another round of eye rolls and sarcastic protests rumble through the room.

"I don't have a talent," Joy protests. "Not one I care to share publicly, anyway."

"You've got six hours to make one up." Art heads out of the room. "Can't wait." His sinister chuckle follows him to the kitchen.

The only thing I feel like doing right now is going back to bed.

It's my brother's birthday.

For the last few years, this day has come and gone like the rest of my family's birthdays—another gloriously numb day I have to get through.

But today, it's different. Elliott's brought back so many memories. Not only do I keep envisioning my twenty-year old self chasing after him, I see my brother by his side, giving us both shit about it.

The ache is bone deep. Prozac can't deaden it. Not today.

I wonder if Elliott remembers. From my vantage point, it doesn't seem like it. He's the same as he's been every day—the picture of calm in a storm, offering support to his coworkers, regardless if they ask, warming the room with quiet humor, standing back and letting everyone else shine, even when he's the shiniest ornament on the tree by far.

He plays with Avery's kid, inherently understanding when she needs a break. He jokes around with his boss, knowing that Skip's beyond worried about these games. He's friendly and nice to his ex-girlfriend, never broadcasting the annoyance I know is there.

Part of me wants to congratulate him. *You've grown into such an amazing man, Eli St. James.* But, I've always known he'd end up like this—wise, light, loose, comfortable in his own skin.

Masculine confidence is so easy to spot. Take Shimura's account guy, Jerry, and his loud mouth and out-of-proportion muscles. That guy has zero confidence.

Alan's another perfect example—his unsubtle desperation and dogged determination to chase after me isn't the least bit attractive. Not to mention, it's wearing incredibly thin. And it's constructing an even thicker wall between Elliott and me.

No, except for the feverish moments my ex and I have spent in private these past few days, one might suspect he hasn't a care in the world.

As usual today, my performance is stellar. It's all smiles and pats on the back and words of encouragement to my sincerely untalented staff, as they practice for the three-ring circus tonight.

No one is taking the pitch seriously anymore. Not even Skip. But tonight's important. Shimura's only a point behind us.

After dinner, we gather in the lodge's theater. Eli ends up in front with his boss, and Alan sits next to my staff a few seats down. This lands me between Avery and Sabrina.

We settle in the leather recliners, each of us with a tall glass of liquid encouragement to soothe the sting of humiliation we're about to undergo for the sake of Proton's amusement.

Burt holds up an electronic box. "Picked this dealie up at a Hollywood charity auction. Applause meter. Points will be awarded based on the audience's reaction."

"Hear that, Samurai?" Skip says. "Every one of you better scream your faces off."

"Once you see my act," Avery says, "you won't have to fake those screams."

I snicker. "Couldn't be any worse than mine."

She shifts her sleepy kid in her lap. "Want to bet?"

"Like, I'm pretty sure I've got you all beat," Sabrina says glumly, two seats down.

Joy turns around from her seat in front of us. "Just wait, bitches, you haven't seen nothing yet." Her flat delivery makes us all squeal with laughter.

Avery sighs happily. "Don't tell my boss, but I'm having a blast."

"I heard that," Skip shouts from the front row. "Stop having fun and focus."

Malcolm prances up to the microphone and taps it with a remote control. "First up—Preeti Deshpande." He flicks a button and a Bollywood beat bumps through the theater.

Clad in a bathrobe, Preeti moves to the stage and mumbles what must be a few choice Hindi curse words. Her robe falls in a puddle to the floor and male gasps sound out around us.

Dressed in a traditional beaded bra top and a sheer sarong, Shimura's intern blows away the audience with her belly dancing skills. Her hips seem to move without the rest of her body and her long black hair, unleashed from her tight bun for the first time, drapes down her back and touches the floor as she arches back and grinds her abs to the beat.

After Preeti's performance, Skip flies out of his seat. "Brava! Brava!" Then comically, he sprints to the front, grabs her robe and covers her up like a worried father.

Christine is called up next. Big surprise, she sings a hymn.

Duffy casts dirty shadow puppets on the theater screen for a few laughs.

Stanley does a sign language number. Of course no one knows what he's saying, so it's a complete flop.

Avery's turn is next. Her son clings to her neck and wraps his legs around her. "Get down, honey," she says gently.

It's clear from the burst of red in his cheeks that that will happen over his dead body. Nervously laughing, she carries him to the front, balanced on her hips.

She struggles to unfold a piece of paper then speaks close to the microphone. "A toddler haiku." She clears her throat, and in a hip-hoppy rhythm she recites the poem. "No, no, no, no, no, no, no, no, no, no, no, no, no, no, no, no, no."

"Ha!" Sam applauds loudly.

No one else seems to get it.

Avery sends Sam a twinkling smile of gratitude that their humor is on the same wavelength. She kisses her son's forehead. "Ready for bed?"

"No!" he shouts, and Sam loses it again.

Avery makes her way back to the seat, and Wang is on next.

He does a completely unimpressive back flip, bows and walks back to his seat before anyone has a chance to react.

I'm on next, and my stomach drops to my knees. I whistle to my dogs and square my shoulders. Down to the front I go. I line up the boys and pull the treats out of my pocket. Before I begin, my gaze shifts to the front row.

Eli is stretched out and watching with interest.

I lick my lips and begin. "There was a man who had a dog and Bingo was his naaam-o. B-i-n-g"—I point to L.L. He barks and I give him a treat. "B-i-n-g"—I point to Trippy. He barks and I throw him a treat. And I continue down this humiliating path until all of the dogs have barked twice and the song is over.

Once more I slide a glance at Eli. His blue eyes are sparkling as brightly as his grin.

But it's Alan's applause that's the loudest. *That douche.*

I stomp back to my seat and flop back in the recliner with a loud smack.

Shimura's developer, Sam, swaggers up to the stage next.

Malcolm presses the remote and music thumps.

What happens next leaves the females in the audience squeezing their thighs together.

The man whips off his shirt and throws it into the crowd. Underneath that long john shirt is a carved physique, covered in ink.

I would describe his dance moves as *Magic Mike*-ish, but he's far hotter than the dude in that movie.

At the end of his performance, Malcolm runs up and hugs his sweaty body. "Thank you. Oh, God! Thank you."

Next to me, Avery's biting her knuckle. "Hold my kid." She plops him in Preeti's lap.

"Where are you going?" asks the intern.

"To masturbate," she replies, slightly out of breath.

No one bats an eye in our row of women, including righteous Christine. No one can deny the sexual inferno that just burned up the stage.

Sam receives the first ten on the applause meter. And the men aren't making a sound.

Skip strolls up onstage next and performs an unintentionally side-splitting comedy routine. He impersonates Ronald Reagan, Jack Nicholson, Tom Hanks, and Elvis, giving each celebrity ridiculous lines. His Ron Burgundy slash Will Ferrell impression has Burt and Art holding their sides, laughing so hard no sound comes out. "You're a smelly pirate hooker. Why don't you go back to your home on Whore Island?" And he delivers it all with a deadpan face, which makes it all the funnier.

I'm giggling and snorting, and it feels so good.

And then Elliott struts up front. I hold my breath and watch him drag empty buckets and cans and place them in a circle around a stool. He yanks a pair of drumsticks out of his back pocket—where he got them is a mystery—and he signals to Malcolm to start the music.

A Phil Collins karaoke rendition of "In The Air Tonight" blares over the speakers.

My heart slams against my chest. That song was my brother's favorite. He used to blast it in the car when he rode up the mountain to go snowboarding.

He remembers.

A wave of emotion blindsides me—grief and gratitude, love and anger. What do I feel? What do I do with this man?

Eli's voice is deep and breathy, just like it was in my brother's band a million years ago.

Joy whoops and screams and holds up a lighter.

The St. James sexy smirk curls up. It's vagina-shattering.

At the drum solo part, he sits on the stool and bangs on the buckets like they're a deluxe kit.

Goose bumps rise on the back of my neck.

He thinks this is funny. I think it's sexy as fuck.

And yet, I find it horribly sad.

While the men shout, "Yeah, dude!" and pump their fists in the air, and the women sway to the music and pretend to scream like rabid fans, I stay frozen in my seat, biting my lips hard so I won't cry.

Sabrina sighs. "God, I miss him."

"Me, too," I whisper, but she doesn't hear me.

Eli glances at me, and his smile fades out with the music.

At the end, I applaud like crazy. He deserves it.

The rest of the performances go by in a flurry. I can no longer pay attention.

Burt and Art announce Shimura as the winner.

Like a zombie, I stand and wander out of the room.

Art grabs my arm on the way out. "Hey, Charlotte." He pulls me over to the side. "I haven't had a chance to chat with you today. How you hanging in there?"

"Huh?"

"It's Patrick's birthday, right?"

I slump over and suck in a breath. A sob is building, threatening to break free. I've become so fragile in the last few days.

Art squeezes me into a bear hug. The pressure of his mass blocks the onslaught of grief, and I'm able to compose myself again.

"Never gets easier, does it?"

I don't answer.

"I'm sorry, sugar. We're always here if you want to talk. How you doing otherwise? Having fun?"

"Sure." *Did that sound peppy enough?*

"Burt and I are having a blast. Can't remember the last time we've had this much fun."

I placate him. "I'm glad."

He pats me softly. "If you feel like talking later, we'll be up, probably going over the video from tonight." A hearty guffaw barks out as he walks away.

I wander back to my room weighted down with feelings. I miss numbness.

On the way, Elliott steps out from the shadows. "You okay, Chicken?"

THIRTY-TWO

Eli Checks the Time

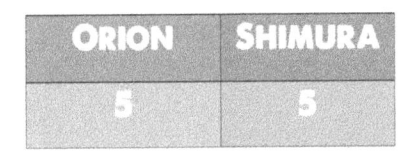

ORION	SHIMURA
5	5

Survival Tip: *You cannot see closed fractures. Symptoms include: severe pain aggravated by movement, tenderness, and swelling.*

Eli's Mixtape: Lo Moon, "Loveless - Edit"

THIS TIME OF YEAR, I usually head to a roof somewhere and drink a six-pack of beer in Patrick's honor.

I miss my friend.

Patrick and I shared a connection that went beyond most friendships. We were more like brothers.

I wait for Charlie at the bottom of the stairs. "You okay, Chicken?"

A rare sight cuts into me—her frown. This is the first time she's let go of that artificial smile.

"Can I show you something?"

She nods and follows me to my room, where she sits on my bed while I dig in my suitcase.

I find her brother's watch and hand it to her. "You should have this."

"Where did you get that?"

"He gave it to me. Before the Olympics. Told me it'd bring me good luck."

I unfurl her fist and place it in her hand.

She handles it as if it's an ancient artifact then lifts it to her nose and smells it.

I chuckle.

"What?"

"I love how you smell everything."

Her shoulders round, and the watch dangles off her finger.

"How do you do it, Charlie? How do you live without them?"

She collapses back on the bed and stares up at the skylight. "I'm not sure I *am* living."

I turn to my side. "What happened after I left? How did you get through it?"

Her dogs jump in bed with us, and we squeeze our bodies together to make room. We don't touch. We just look.

I want to kiss her and hold her. But I don't feel worthy. How could I, after what I did?

When she doesn't answer me, I tell her the story about the watch. "Remember when your dad gave Patrick that?"

"He thought he was such a stud with that thing," she says. "It drove me crazy. He was always flashing it at people. I kept telling him he was going to get mugged one day."

"The day he got it we went boarding, and he kept screwing around with it. He dropped it off the chairlift. I had to stop him from jumping off. He kept shouting all those made up swear words of his."

"Ass-licking donkey fucker?"

"Something like that." I shake my head. "We spent, I-shit-you-not, two hours looking for that thing. We're on our hands and knees in the snow, and this hot chick skis up to us with the watch in her hands. 'Are you looking for this?' Long story short, Pat ditches me for this woman, and I have to take the bus back to Boulder. I was so pissed."

"Ugh, the bus is the worst."

"I didn't hear from him for two days. Then he showed up at my house, bragging that he'd spent the 'best days' of his life in bed with that chick, and that the watch had 'magical pussy powers.'"

She wrinkles her nose. "Gross."

"But then the chick's husband came home and nearly killed him." I laugh, and it hurts. "'Doesn't sound lucky to me,' I told him."

"'I didn't die,' he told me. 'If that's not luck, I don't know what is.' He was always so positive." I sigh. "Except when it came to you."

She blinks back her tears. "What do you mean?"

"He never wanted me around you."

"That's not true. He loved you."

"He did, but he didn't want us together. That's why I left." A bomb ticks inside me. Am I about to confess?

She strokes the straps of the watch then hands it back to me. "I can't take this. He gave it to you. I don't really need magic pussy powers."

"True." I stroke her St. Bernard's velvety ear, wondering if I should back up and tell her everything. The depth of despair behind her airy humor doesn't fool me. Do we need to do this now? Do I have to tell her?

She looks down at the dog and back at me. "It doesn't bother you he's in the bed?"

"I love dogs. I'd get one, but I live in a tiny place and work a lot. It wouldn't be fair."

"Do you like your job?"

"I do. I like the people." This small talk is making my skin itch.

I reach out and cup her cheek.

We hug and stay that way, just breathing, until someone knocks on my door.

"If it's that fucker, Alan..." I shoot out of bed and fling open the door.

In front of me, in a red negligée with her tits completely exposed, stands Sabrina, drunk as hell, trying to strike a sexy pose in the doorway.

"Aren't you going to invite me in?" Her lashes flutter.

The cogs in my male brain get stuck. I can't seem to formulate a sentence or find a solution to this harrowing problem.

Charlie pushes past me. "'Night, Elliott. You two have fun."

"No," I say. "Wrong one." *Wrong one? What am I, Avery's son?*

Sabrina rubs her arms and bounces. "Can I come in?"

My gaze unwillingly shifts to her hard nipples. I groan. Sabrina has the most beautiful tits. I slap my cheeks. "Yeah, we need to talk."

I motion to the bed for her to have a seat.

She spread-eagles on top, which has the complete opposite effect it should have.

"Get up, Sabrina." I help her sit. "Why do you do this to yourself?"

"I know. I drank so much."

"Not the wine, me. Why do you keep this up?"

Melodramatic drunken tears pour out of mascara-smeared eyes. "Because I love you."

Oh, God. I dry her tears with my sleeve. "No, you don't. I've never given you a reason to love me." I tilt her chin. "When we got together, I told you no strings. And you said, 'I'm game, Eli.' Remember?"

"I thought you would change your mind."

"Men are simple creatures, babe. We pretty much tell it like it is. I never wanted to hurt you, and I'm sorry if I did, but you and I"—I wave a hand back and forth—"this isn't going to happen. Not now. Not ever."

"It's her, isn't it?" she bawls. "What's-her-face? Charlotte."

My agreement bubbles to the surface, but I swallow it back. I don't have a clue what's going on between Charlie and me. Even if that were it, I still wouldn't be with Sabrina. "I care for you, I really do. But not the way you want."

She buries her face under the covers. "I'm such an idiot."

"No."

"I am. I'm so stupid. Everyone makes fun of me."

I'm already tired of this. "You're a good person. You're beautiful. And you're kind. There's someone out there for you." It's sickening, the cheese coming out of my mouth. "It'll happen. You've just gotta stop chasing the wrong guys." *Namely, me.*

Her forearm folds over her eyes. "Ugh. I feel so stupid. Please don't tell anyone I did this."

"Mum's the word," I tell her.

The most pathetic smile pushes past her puffy lips. "Thank you for being honest with me."

This is an odd statement, considering I've been honest with her all along. But she's pretty wasted.

She keeps smiling, and for a minute, I worry she's going to pass out in my bed. Then, much to my relief, she wobbles to her feet and weaves toward the door. "See you tomorrow," she slurs and closes the door behind her.

Whoa. A lot just happened in the last five minutes. I need to zone out. Or meditate. Or masturbate. I don't know, something.

What I end up doing is praying. I'm not religious. I never pray. But the moment feels right. I make this ridiculous deal with whomever I'm praying to. If I can somehow make it up to

Charlie, somehow make her happy, maybe I could forgive myself.

Heaviness covers me while the snow slides down the skylight outside.

I hug my pillow, wishing it were Charlie and her pack of dogs.

Then I fall asleep, dreaming about Patrick and his stupid magic pussy watch. In my dream, she comes back to me. And for a while, I float in absolute bliss, before everything turns black.

THIRTY-THREE

Eli Falls Hard

Survival Tip: *A clear trail will make carrying baggage much easier.*

Eli's Mixtape: Kaleo, "Way Down We Go"

THE FOLLOWING MORNING AT BREAKFAST, Burt informs the group that he has special plans for us.

Groans and moans detonate around the table, mostly coming from my coworkers.

Truth is, Shimura's team spirit is shot. Sure, we're tied with Orion, but we're also sick of these games.

At the table, two sets of eyes burn holes through my skull—emerald green lasers on the left and brown sugar daggers on the right.

I focus on the darker pair—the pair with one lid fluttering closed over a hilarious attempt at a stink-eye. I laugh out loud and the glare grows hotter.

What's the use? She's not going to believe I sent Sabrina packing last night. I fold my hands behind my head and sigh.

Art spreads his legs in a macho stance and delivers the rules. "Today, you're going geocaching. Each team will receive a GPS tracker and a backpack full of supplies. Each cache contains clues to the final destination—Proton's private yurt."

More groans.

"Bunch of wussies," Burt mumbles.

"We're going to try something different today," Art chimes in. "You'll be working in pairs with a member from the other team."

I slump down in my chair. Watch those dicks pair me up with Alan.

"How long is the hike?" Wang asks.

"It'll take you most of the day to get there. But there's a pot of gold at the end of the rainbow. Our hut's in the protected wilderness, next to the most pristine hot springs you've ever seen. This ain't no overcrowded amusement park, folks. The only other guests you'll probably run into is a bunch of wildlife."

Sabrina raises her hand.

I brace myself for the stupidity about to exit her mouth.

"How do we get there?" she asks.

"Snowshoes," Art tells her.

"Malcolm!" Burt yells. "Bring out the list."

Donning a floral scarf and a Camp Proton sweatshirt, Malcolm sighs dramatically and flounces to the front of the room with a clipboard. "When I call your names, go stand by your partner and bossman will give you your gear. Team one: Stanley and Sabrina. Team two: Skip and Joy…" He names a few more pairs and then calls out Alan and Preeti.

I unclench my pant leg then reclench it when I realize the only pair left is Charlie and I.

I squint-smile at Burt.

He squints-smiles back.

A ridge twitches in Charlie's jaw. She is not amused with her godfather's hijinks.

Nor am I.

Still, I can't ignore the spark that just ignited inside me. The whole day to ourselves. So many ways this could go. I focus on the sexual path. Why? Because I'm a masochist.

Loaded down with our equipment, Burt hands me a map at the door. "Have fun, Beav."

I tear the paper out of his grasp and study it.

Charlie arrives by my side with her dogs.

"Sure that's a good idea, bringing them?" I ask. "What if Julius has another episode?"

"They'll tear up the lodge otherwise. Bad separation anxiety." Without another word, she takes off on her own.

Apparently, we're taking the other path today. The rocky, grudge-y path.

Neither of us are in a particularly chatty mood. So we crunch through the snow for over an hour, in search of the red canisters containing our first clue.

Finally, we discover the first one hanging from a post. We unroll the next map and continue on in silence.

The air's too fresh, like it's about to snow. There's no indication how much longer we have, and there's no way to find out. All we have is the GPS. No walkie-talkies. No phones. No way to call for help. This is an incredibly stupid idea on Proton's part. They should know better.

I grew up in the mountains. I know how dangerous it is out here. Sweat mixed with chilly wind and wet snow is the perfect recipe for hypothermia. It's a good thing we're both experienced hikers.

For the next half-mile, I focus on the beautiful scenery. Namely, her ass. A memory of hiking with her in college pops up—her ahead of me, holding my hand, quietly taking in nature.

She stops and calls out the coordinates on the GPS. "This is it, right?"

A white jackrabbit bursts out from behind a tree and scurries away.

One of her dogs takes off after it and bounds up a steep incline.

"Shit!" She unloads her pack and drops it next to a tree.

"I'll go," I tell her. Her shoulder has to be killing her after wearing that heavy thing.

"No!" she snaps. "Just stay here."

I ignore her and climb the peak.

This infuriates her. "I told you not to come."

"You might need a hand."

"I don't need you." The double meaning of this is not lost.

I stop and stare at her. "Why is it such a big deal for you to ask for help?"

She marches on, her fists probably clenched in little balls in those mittens of hers.

We follow the tracks to the top. It's an incredible workout. My knee burns, especially since I'm still wearing my pack.

At the top, her mutt is digging under a tree on the edge of a cliff.

The view is insane—saw-toothed white ridges jutting up above black trees. We're close to timberline—around 11,000 feet.

In the distance, the fourteeners, Grays and Torreys, stretch up to the sun. It's staggering how high up we are.

Up here, where the air is thin and the view expands for hundreds of miles, it's humbling, like a religious experience. This is where church should take place, out here in this cathedral.

I silently give thanks for the creation of this magnificence.

Meanwhile, Charlie's having a helluva time trying to drag L.L. away from that tree. Now the other three are in on the chase.

I amble over to give her hand, and then stop in my tracks. There's a rumble beneath my feet. "Don't move," I whisper. "Don't even breathe."

Crack! Bang! Whoosh! And then, *wham!* All that's left is white and a tiny whimper above me.

Know what I was thinking in that instant? Hope I die first.

THIRTY-FOUR

Charlie Lets Go

This is it. I finally get to see my family again. I just have to let go.

Snap! I drop an inch.

Searing pain stabs my hand. I need to rest my arm and get my mitten off. Then I can hold on for a bit longer.

I try to switch my grip, but my injured shoulder won't let me.

I stare down at what meets me thousands of feet below. There are no giant mattresses or nets or trampolines—just boulders and skeletal trees.

A noise leaks out from a foreign place inside me, animalistic almost, like a whimpering dog. It *is* a whimpering dog. *My dogs!* Their cries of distress give me a burst of strength and allow me to cling a little longer.

Why can't I let go? I'm not ready. I need more time.

"Charlie, let go!"

"I can't!"

"I've got you. Let go!"

"No! Not yet!"

"Goddammit, Chicken, let go of that goddamn branch! I've got you!"

Everything gives out—the branch, my strength, my arm—and I give in.

Life rushes by in a translucent blur, and all at once, I'm terrifyingly free.

THIRTY-FIVE

Eli Dies

December 2005

I DIED three times in two weeks.

The night before my first death, snow dumped fresh powder on the mountain, and while it softly piled up on the slopes, I was cozy under a pile of covers, buried inside Charlie.

Earlier that evening, we'd celebrated my qualification for the Olympic snowboard trials. In a few weeks, I would be leaving to train in Turin, Italy, with Team USA.

She didn't know it, but I was going to propose before I left.

But first, I had to tell her brother I was in love with her.

Patrick had been my best friend since the age of eleven. We were in Scouts together. We drank our first beer together. We smoked our first pack of smokes, experimented with drugs, watched porn, and even jacked off together one weird night in his basement.

We never went anywhere without each other. In junior high, we played in a band and snowboarded all nine months of the season.

He was the one who got me into racing. And his family's support was the reason I excelled at the sport. They were the ones clanging the cowbell at the finish line. My family was too busy.

The Sullivans were everything to me. They were the parents I wanted. And I didn't want to lose them.

For years, I'd had a crush on Patrick's wild tomboy sister, but he made it clear she was off limits. Clear, as in, he threatened to slice off my balls if I touched her.

Part of his reasoning was justified. He was worried if something happened between Charlie and me it would affect our friendship. That worried me too, quite honestly.

I tried to forget her by dating others, but that just made me look worse in her brother's eyes. He saw me *slam, bam, thank you ma'am* so many women that he was convinced I'd do the same to his sister.

I concentrated on snowboarding instead and started winning every race. A lot of that had to do with Charlie standing at the finish line with those "Loser" signs. It became a running joke with us, because I always won.

Even though my mind was always on racing, my heart was always with her. And her brother, for that matter. I loved them both.

I was so torn. What if falling in love with her meant losing my best friend?

When Charlie and I finally got together, I begged her to keep it a secret. I wanted to be sure we would last.

Also, it was kind of fun, sneaking around. It made things more exciting.

At the end of our first year, I won the nationals and qualified for the Olympic trials.

It's difficult to explain how satisfying it is to be madly in love and reach the pinnacle of your career at the same time. It's like the biggest high in the world.

A week later, the day of my first death, I stood on top of that snowy peak, and I shouted to the world. "I am God!"

Sounds cocky, but that's how I felt. Like I was one step away from ruling Heaven.

I let go and flew down the slopes, my body flowing, my soul soaring, and my board carving up the mountain.

And then I caught a weird edge and slammed into a tree.

At the time, I thought it was the worst pain ever. I was wrong.

After I came out of surgery that night with my leg in a cast, Charlie wouldn't leave my side.

"It's okay, if you cry," she said. "I won't tell anyone."

I laughed a little at her sweetness. Most people only saw her tough exterior. But I'd seen enough of her vulnerable side to know she was as girly as they came.

"I'm not going to cry, Chicken," I told her. "You'll make fun of me."

She jerked back in horror. "I would never do that!"

I squeezed her hand. "I probably wouldn't have made it through the trials anyway. No big deal. I'll live."

When I'd said that, I really believed it. I'd graduate from college and get on with my life. I'd take a job in graphic design, maybe become a snowboard coach. I was only twenty-one. I had my whole life ahead of me. Hell, maybe I'd try out for the Olympics again.

They let me out of the hospital two days later, and I went home with her. When I tried to walk on my own, it hit me —the loss.

I couldn't help but remember my arrogance on the mountain. Someone had knocked me down a peg and reminded me not to take things for granted.

For the first time ever, I slipped under the dead weight of depression. I wouldn't eat or get out of bed. I didn't want to talk about it.

But Charlie wouldn't let me wander through the dark alone.

She made it her mission to get me out of bed. And she did it by taunting me.

She bought me a walker and an alert button for the bathroom. "In case you fall and can't get up," she told me. "Now that you're old and handicapped—"

"I'm not old or handicapped."

"Well, I just assumed…since you won't get out of bed. Oh, by the way, I called Dad to build a ramp for you, and I checked into a handicapped sticker for the Jeep."

I got up and limped over to her. "Do not call your father."

"Look at you!" she said with a devious grin. "You don't even need a cane."

"All right, I get the point."

"Good. Because you need to get in the shower."

By the end of the week, I was damn near at seventy-five percent. I felt good enough to let my girl ride me. In fact, I felt so damn good I refused to answer the phone calls.

Then her phone started ringing.

She stopped moving. "Something's wrong," she said.

"Hand me the phone."

"No."

"Chicken."

"Something's wrong."

I held her for a moment longer then reached for her cell, just to prove her wrong.

I'll spare you the details of what happened next. After all, you'd have to be a sadist to want to hear about her entire family dying in a car accident.

The only thing I will tell you is that thirty minutes before the call from the police came, Patrick texted me this:

I know Ur seeing my sister, U asshole. Mom and Dad and I are coming to beat Ur assets.

It's hard to laugh at a typo when it's the last text you ever get from your best friend.

On the way to beat my ass, they lost control and crashed through a guardrail and hit a semi.

I killed the Sullivans.

A week after that, Charlie killed me.

Where do you go when you die? For me it was the opposite of Heaven: New York City.

THIRTY-SIX

Eli Kills

Survival Tip*: Deep wounds may have to be drained or reopened to prevent infection.*

Eli's Mixtape: The Dead Weather, "60 Feet Tall"

ON A LEDGE no more than three feet wide by six feet long, I caught Charlie in my arms.

Between you and me? I didn't think I could do it. Or that *she* could do it.

I stumble to my knees and set her down. For a brief expanse of time that feels like light years, we exist on the ledge, inhaling and exhaling, grasping each other, trying to fathom the unfathomable, marveling that we survived this extraordinary peril together without serious injury.

"Are you hurt?" is the first phrase out of my mouth.

She's shaking violently and darting glances everywhere.

"Charlie." I hold her chin in place. "Are you hurt?"

Wild terror seizes her expression. "Where are my dogs?"

Shit! I didn't even think about them.

She calls out their names, and the little guy with the bad eye prances out from a crevasse hidden underneath a wall of ice. It's amazing he lived.

It's amazing *we* lived.

We fell a good thirty feet. Evidently, we were standing on a snow cornice, and there was nothing to support it.

It must have formed during the ice storm, along with the glacier covering the cliff. Now there is no way to get back up without ice climbing gear.

The tree above fell over, and by some miracle, didn't crush us.

I don't know how Charlie managed to hold onto the branch as long as she did, without pulling it over on top of her.

Overhead, I spot two furry heads poking over the edge. "There are the other two."

A whoosh of air blasts out of her. "Thank God. L.L.? Are you up there, too?"

Whimpers spring up from below.

We peer over the cliff. Eight feet down, stuck on an even thinner ledge than ours, the St. Bernard is shaking and whining, unable to move without killing himself.

Charlie crouches like she's actually capable of leaping down to save that hundred-and-fifty pound goliath by herself.

I grab her elbow. "You're not going anywhere."

"I'm not leaving him down there."

"I'll get him." No idea how I'm going to accomplish this, but *hey*, I just survived an avalanche, might as well commit suicide.

My backpack lies to my left, still half-buried in the snow. I dig it out and dump out a zippered bag with the words Proton Sports Survival Kit monogrammed on front. Inside is the following:

- 1 rain poncho
- 1 space blanket

- 1 mini-flashlight
- 1 signaling mirror
- 1 whistle
- 1 emergency fishing kit
- 4, 12" cords and plastic stakes to make the space blanket into a shelter
- 2 carabiners
- 2 hand warmer gel packs
- 1 all-in-one tool
- 1 fire starter rod
- 6 chemically treated tinder balls
- 1 first aid kit, with gauze, tape, moleskin, bug spray, sunscreen, and three bandages
- 3 freeze-dried meals
- 1 packet of beef jerky
- 1 packet of energy chews
- 10 water treatment tablets
- 1 half-filled water bottle

We also have one trek pole and three damaged snowshoes.

I huff and stuff everything back in the bag. "No rope, no axe, no shovel, no goddamned walkie-talkies. What the hell were they thinking?" It's an absurd question at this point. "And why did they pack those meals and nothing to cook them in?"

"All of that was in my pack." She rubs her shoulder and glances down at her dog. "What are we going to do?"

I stare at our meager supplies. "I don't even have a hat."

She hands me her red knit beanie. "Use mine. I have a hood."

I don't take it. I just keep staring at the things that may or may not keep us alive for another two or three days max.

With her hurt shoulder and my hurt knee, we're not exactly freehand ice climbers. And there's the other matter—her dogs, which knowing her, she'd sacrifice her own life to save them.

In other words, it's looking bleak, and hauling her dog up to us is looking even bleaker.

I tell her like it is. "Without a harness, I could slip and die."

Deep creases line her forehead. "I know. Don't do it." There is such despair in her tone it overshadows every obstacle we're facing.

"Let me see your scarf," I say.

She unravels it and hands it over.

I dangle it over the edge. It covers half the distance. I pull it back up and drag my hand down my beard. "We can try to make a harness out of the space blanket and your scarf," I say. "But we don't have anything to anchor it. Or anything to make a pulley system."

"What if we cut the blanket into strips and tied it in knots?"

I dip my chin and give her an are-you-kidding-me look.

Then I notice the trek pole again. I pick it up and lower it over the edge. With the space blanket, scarf, and pole, it'll reach the dog. "It might work if I had something to anchor us."

"You," she says. "You hold the pole and I'll get him. I weigh less. It should be me. Then he won't get scared. I'll put your backpack on and we can tie the scarf to that and the other end to the lanyard on your pole. I'll slide down and cover him with the blanket. Then I'll push him up, while you pull."

"And what about you? How are you going to get back up?"

"I'm an excellent climber, better than you."

With a harsh look, I tell her I'm in no mood for her risky, competitive behavior.

"I'll tie the space blanket around me like a harness and attach the scarf, and that way, if I slip on the way down, you've got me."

"I don't like this."

But apparently, I don't have a say in the matter, since she's already wrapping the space blanket around her waist like a diaper.

I won't bore you with the events that transpired next, like my arms almost snapping in half, or her almost falling off the edge, or the struggle her dog gave us, or the bald spots I gave him by yanking him up by his fur, or the seventeen tries it took her to get back up—suffice it to say, we're all together now, on the upper ledge, safe.

Safe, as in we have a little more time before we either starve or freeze to death.

As if the universe read my mind, snow blows down from the sky in wild, windy swirls.

We waste no time building a shelter. The crevasse between the adjacent cliff is big enough for the four of us to cram inside. We can't lie down in it, and the razor-sharp rocks underneath are no substitute for a bed, but it's better than dying from exposure or frostbite.

Using the broken snowshoe, we pile crusty snow in a wall around the entrance for insulation, and then we drape the space blanket across the opening and tie it down with the tent cords, buried in the snow.

We cut open the backpack and spread it and the rain poncho on the ground, then haul in what little supplies we have.

I then perform the death-defying act of gathering fuel. I pitch the rock, with the scarf attached, over the tree about fifty times before it actually works. Then I hang off it until the branches break off and we manage to gather seven twigs and one limb, that won't last more than an hour.

I would have given up the second time, but Charlie kept egging me on with her terrible rendition of "Eye of the Tiger," in which she substituted the real lyrics with her made-up ones.

"Rising up, slipping on sleet. Eli's fine, and takes chances. Missed the distance, now he's back on his feet. Just a man and his will to surviiiiive. So many times it happens too fast. You trade your scarf in for glory! Don't lose your grip on the dreams of our past. Eli must fight just to keep us alive. And the last known survivor throws his scarf in the night. And I'm watching him faaaaall with the eye of the tiger. Dun! Dun, duh, dun, duh, dun duh!"

Grinning and shaking my head, I start singing along with her.

This is the Charlie I remember—the fighter, the comedian, the enchantress—the woman who makes surviving an avalanche fun.

When the chore is done, it's just after noon, and we find ourselves with nothing to do. So we stand at the edge, and gaze down at the barrenness below.

"It's so pretty up here," she says.

"That it is."

Another long moment passes. "If we get out of here, what's the first thing you want to do?"

"We *are* getting out of here." I can barely believe the optimism that just came out of my mouth. "And the first thing I'm gonna do is make love with you."

She gives me a shy smile. "Really?"

"Yep."

She stuffs her hand in my pocket. "I can't think of anyone else I'd rather be trapped on a mountain with than you."

"I take it you're not pissed at me anymore."

"Hmm?"

"About Sabrina. Last night. I kicked her out after you left, in case you were wondering."

"Poor girl. Even a blind man could see you're not into her."

I draw back a little and lift a brow. "You knew?"

Her gaze turns back to the mountaintops. "Every time she looks at you, you're looking at me."

I squeeze her closer. "If you weren't upset, then what was up with silent treatment? You must have been mad about something."

"I'm not mad. I'm sad." She pauses before clarifying. "I don't know what to do with you or us or this." She ducks out from under my hold and faces me. Her mouth opens and closes. Then she takes a deep breath and starts again.

A shudder rolls over me. We are about to have "the talk." The talk we've been, or rather *I've* been avoiding. The "what happened" talk. The "what now" talk. The talk where I'm forced to come clean.

The first thing she says is, "I'm sorry for cheating on you." Her pitch grows higher, and the words come out faster. "I thought you left me. You didn't tell me where you were going or when you'd be back. I had no one to turn to. That night, I drank a fifth of vodka."

I shield my eyes. I can't watch her do this—the guilt, the pain.

"I don't remember anything about that guy," she says. "I don't remember his name. Or what he looked like. I don't remember anything. He was just a substitute. A plug filling a black void."

I lower my hand and brave a glance. Her lips are trembling and her lashes are wet.

Suddenly, I feel every bruise and scrape from the fall. "It doesn't matter now," I say. "It's over."

"But it's not! Here we are!" She points at her chest. "This isn't just sex for me. I have feelings for you. Scary feelings. And you're just standing there, looking annoyed, not talking to me, being a fucking man."

"I didn't leave you," I say quietly.

She jumps to her feet and screams, "You did! Twice!"

My blood shoots up to my head and pounds against my temples. "I was devastated, Charlie. I lost them, too. *And* my goddamned career. I needed time to process everything. So I handled it poorly. I was twenty-one years old. And then you slept with that guy. You knew about my mom cheating on my dad. How did you think I was going to react? Did you think I was going to stick around for more fun times?"

Her expression calcifies into stone. "I needed you."

"I needed you!"

Tears gurgle up in her voice. "I'm sorry. I was just as young and dumb as you. But you still left. And you didn't tell me you were coming back."

"I left because I killed your family." I slam my eyes shut and listen for her response.

All I hear is my own heartbeat.

THIRTY-SEVEN

Charlie Dates An Amputee

December 2005

SOMETHING TERRIBLE HAPPENED. Elliott hurt his knee, and now he can't go to the Olympics.

I'm really worried about him. He's been so depressed. I don't know what to do. He won't talk to me. I keep telling him he has his whole life ahead of him. The doctor told us he would be fine in a year.

I talked to Weiner about it, and he told me to leave him alone, let him recover on his own time. I begged him to come over and cheer him up, but he said that would be weird since he hasn't come clean about our relationship.

Weiner's pissed Elliott won't stop lying about us. There's no doubt that Loser loves me, but sometimes, I wonder.

But then I remember I haven't opened a car door in his presence since I was ten. And he likes my crazy made-up songs and weird sense of humor. Most of all, he loves me.

I can wait. He'll get better.

I have faith in that Loser. He's the strongest man I know.

THIRTY-EIGHT

Charlie Clings

Eli's Mixtape: Hippie Sabotage, "Your Soul"

"I killed your family."

One by one, snowflakes land on my face and melt. I shiver and wait for him to explain.

When he finally speaks, his voice is so soft and strangled it crashes against me. "Patrick found out about us. Right before the accident, he sent me a text. He was with your mom and dad, said they were all coming to beat my ass."

He pauses and runs his hand through his frozen hair. "Well, actually, he said, 'I'm coming to beat your assets,' but I knew what he meant." He violently rubs his forehead. "Rage driving. They wrecked because of me. I killed them."

I stare at him without blinking. Does he seriously think he caused their accident?

He bounces from foot to foot, scratching his face, rolling his shoulders.

I'm grateful for our imprisonment on top of this godforsaken rock. Otherwise, he'd run away.

Survivor's guilt.

That's what my therapist called it.

"*You believe you're the one who should have died in that wreck.*" She'd stated this as though it were fact.

"That's ridiculous," I told her. "*It was an accident.*"

"*Let's talk about your self-destructive behavior.*" She'd listed the examples. "*The drunk driving. The sex with strangers. The extreme sports. The reckless stunts. When you're not working yourself to death, you're trying to kill yourself.*" She had paused and noted my expression. "*Why are you smiling? Is this funny to you?*"

I feel my lips. They're dry and leathery and curved up. A storm of laughter is brewing in my belly. It's so wrong. I bite my smile off and snort.

"Are you laughing?" he asks.

It's like my head blows off, and my emotions erupt. I collapse on my back and howl. My laughter echoes over the valley. "You fucking idiot!"

And then I cry and wail and moan. It's the first time I've cried about this. And it hurts. *Oh God*, it hurts. My dog frantically licks my hand.

All of a sudden, the tears dry up. I focus on him.

He's pale, like he's going to vomit. And he's frozen in place like a statue.

"You left me, when I needed you the most, because you thought you killed my family?"

Not a peep comes out of him.

I shout at him. "They knew! They always knew. They were just waiting for you to grow a spine and stop sneaking around. Patrick found your stupid engagement ring. They were coming over to celebrate. Don't you remember the pictures of the accident? There were broken champagne bottles all over the highway."

"They knew?"

"Yes! How could they not? My God, Elliott, we fell in love in elementary school. You can't hide that."

Three more times he repeats the words, as if trying to firmly cement them in his mind. And then he fists his hair and tips back his head and roars. "THEY FUCKING KNEW!"

He turns to me, eyes wild with terror. "I've been living a lie for ten years. What the fuck is wrong with me?" His body seems to give out, and he sinks to his knees in the snow.

"And you," he says after a long, tortured moment. "You knew I was going to propose?"

"Patrick always had such a big mouth. He never could keep a secret."

"That son of a bitch." He gapes at me.

I reach for his arm and keep my hand there for a moment. "I blamed myself, too." The past tense is right, because as of this moment, it ends. The guilt. I have no use for it anymore. I forgive myself. I forgive him. I forgive my brother for driving my parents into a semi. And I forgive them for leaving me.

I do this silently, almost as a prayer. I release my pain and give it to the mountains. *Take it away!*

Then I crawl over and lay on top of him. My dogs lay on top of him too.

He grunts. "Are you guys trying to smother me?"

I kiss him softly, delicately, and he hugs me tightly.

"I feel like I should take you to dinner or something," he says. "Like out on a date. Make up for lost time. Start over and get back to where we were."

"Pizza sounds so good right now."

"I know. I'm starving."

I lay my head on his chest and let the rise and fall of his breathing soothe me. "Think we can? Start over?" I ask.

"Do *you*?"

"I don't want to lose you."

He removes his glove and slides his hand under my jacket. His fingers curl around my breasts. He needs skin-to-skin contact.

So do I.

"You never told me what you'd do," he asks, "when we get off this cliff."

"Make love with you, of course."

He grabs my bottom and kisses me. "Good girl." Then he rolls me off and sits up. "What else would you do? Besides hump me?"

I sit back on my hands. "I'd go to Machu Picchu and scatter my family's ashes."

"You still have them?"

"Yeah."

His lips pull back. "That's kind of gross."

"I know. I haven't been ready. It's hard to explain."

"Why Machu Picchu?"

"Remember my dad was big into astronomy? He always wanted to take us there. Apparently, there's some sort of magic stone that does something special during the equinox. We could never get our schedules to work out, so he kept putting it off."

"How come you haven't gone?"

I let out a big breath. "I don't know. Guess I haven't wanted to let them go."

He winds my pigtail around his finger. "I miss them, too. I miss your mom a lot. I could always talk to her about anything."

His words pluck a tight string around my heart. "She loved you, too." I change the subject. "What about your family? Have you seen them, yet?"

He frowns. "They don't know I'm here."

"Are you going there for Christmas?"

"Hadn't planned on it."

"Why?"

"I don't really get along with them. It's been weird between us for a long time."

I stare at him.

"Why're you looking at me like that?"

"Elliott Andrew St. James, your parents are alive and well, and you don't want to see them because of their sex life? What I wouldn't give to argue with my mother again." I'm aware this is a total guilt-trip, but he doesn't seem to get the life-is-too-short bit.

He digs out my red hat and pulls it over his head. "Maybe I'll stop by for Christmas. Surprise them."

"So you don't have any plans for the holidays?"

"No."

"Me, neither. I never do. I hate the holidays."

"I don't really enjoy them myself."

What I'm about to offer next feels like the biggest risk I've ever taken in my life. "Want to spend them with me? We can 'not enjoy' them together."

He smiles. "I'd like that."

We hold hands and gaze at the wilderness for a moment. "We have to get out of here."

"I know," he says. "Let's hang tight for a bit until they figure out we're gone."

"The weather's getting worse. I'm worried about my dogs up there."

"They'll be fine."

"Maybe I should throw a beef jerky up there?"

"You and those dogs." He stands and offers me a hand. "Come on. Let's get in the shelter."

THIRTY-NINE

Eli Saves A Dog

Survival Tip: *If you decide that rescue is unlikely, leave clear signs behind so searchers have an indication of your route.*

Eli's Mixtape: Portugal. The Man, "Don't Look Back in Anger"

THE REST OF THE AFTERNOON, we fill each other in on the last ten years of our lives. I tell her about my music career and about my former rock star roommate, Elias.

"That guy is totally my celebrity crush. What's he like?"

"Quiet. Considerate. Funny. In love. He's got a girlfriend. She's cool. Makes him happy."

"I read about her. Wasn't she a drug addict?"

"Yeah, she's clean now though."

She asks what I do in my spare time.

I tell her a few things. And that's it—the story of Eli St. James. No crazy adventures. No real legacy. No struggles. What happened to me? How did I get so boring?

From what it sounds like, her life hasn't been all that different from mine. Other than the extreme sports, all she does is work.

The sun disappears early and leaves us shivering in the shelter. I'm snuggled around Charlie, and she's curled around her dogs.

The space blanket flaps and snaps in the wind. I fight the urge to fire up a tinder ball. The package says it'll burn up to four hours, but it's going to get a lot colder later on.

She sneaks her dogs a piece of a jerky when she thinks I'm not looking.

"I saw that."

"They're hungry."

"We might have to eat them." I wish I were kidding.

She smacks my leg. "Bite your tongue."

I scratch her big mutt's ears. "Better fatten you up, boy."

"You know what's crazy?" she says. "I'm having fun. It reminds me of when we used to go camping."

"It *is* kind of fun. In a really fucked-up way."

Later, we doze off. The dogs wake us up in the dark, barking like maniacs. I grab the flashlight and peel back the blanket.

A family of bighorn sheep stares at us. Then they dart down the mountainside.

"Holy shit!" I jump out of the shelter and watch them. "We should have lassoed them with your scarf and rode them down to the bottom."

She bursts out laughing.

I do too.

All of a sudden, I hear something. "Shh! Listen." The sound of snowmobiles nears.

We jump up and down and scream for help.

The engines cut off. "Charlotte? Bearded Clam? You down there?"

"Burt! Down here!" Charlie cries.

"Thank God. You hurt?"

"No! We're okay."

"All right," he says. "We're gonna haul you out of there with the snowmobiles and a harness." He lowers down a rope.

"My dogs are down here!"

"Is that where the big guy is? You got the little guy, too?"

"Yeah, he's down here."

"Eli, think you can hold onto him?" Burt asks.

A hundred and fifty pound dog? No way. But then I take stock of Charlie's worried expression. "I'll try."

"Too bad I don't have the tranquilizer gun," he laments.

"You have a tranquilizer gun?" I ask.

"For bears."

"Your godfather scares me," I say out loud.

"Charlie first," Burt shouts. "Stuff the little pooch in your jacket."

She tugs on the rope. "Got 'em."

The engines turn back on. On the way up, she crashes against the glacier about twenty times.

I'm totally going to kill her dog.

When it's my turn, Burt doesn't drop the harness. "Night, Beaver Boy!"

"What the—? Man, I am not in a joking mood."

"I'm just messing with you." He lowers the harness. "Get in, hippie."

Somehow I don't drop the dog. Instinctively, he lies perfectly still in my arms, as if knowing it was a life or death situation.

We make it to the top alive, albeit banged up and bruised.

The first thing I do is charge over to Burt with my dukes up. "You stupid son of a bitch. What were you thinking leaving us out here with no communication?"

"What happen to the avalanche beacon?" Art asks.

"What avalanche beacon?"

"On the GPS?"

"There was an avalanche beacon on that thing?" Charlie asks.

"And a walkie-talkie."

"We lost it in the avalanche!" I shout.

"Dumbass," Burt grumbles.

"How'd you find us?" Charlie asks.

"The dogs wandered back to the lodge. We followed the cache route and saw Charlie's pack. On a hunch, we rode up here. Good thing we did."

"Aw, my boys saved our lives."

"They sure did. Jump on. We'll get you up to the yurt."

I protest. "We need to go back to the lodge."

"The yurt's two clicks up. The lodge is a good hour drive. It's best to warm you up and get you fed. We'll take you back in the morning."

I can't argue with that. My blood feels thick, like I'm on the verge of hypothermia.

On the way to the hut, I'm stuck with the beast and Burt, and my butt hangs over the edge of the seat.

A short while later, we arrive at our destination—two glowing yurts in the middle of the forest. A stream babbles nearby, and there's a tinge of sulfur in the air. It must be the hot springs he was talking about earlier.

When we make it inside, everyone's half-naked and seated around a table, playing strip poker. No one looks up from their cards.

Christine is passed out on the floor with a bottle of wine next to her.

"Took you long enough," Joy says.

Charlie looks like she's about to decapitate her designer. "That's because we were trapped at the bottom of a cliff!"

"I bet," Sam says with a shitting-eating grin.

"No really," I say. "We were in an avalanche."

"Buried deep, eh?" Jerry bucks his hips.

"Shut it, Jerry," I growl.

Alan weaves out of the bathroom in his boxer shorts and

heads straight for Charlie. "There you are! I was worried sick." He hugs her.

She pries his hands off. "I can see that. How much have you had to drink?"

He pinches a finger and thumb and closes one eye. "Little bit." His hammered bloodshot gaze shifts over to me. "Was he with you?"

I wave my fingers. "Right here, asshole. And yes, we were together." I'm guessing he still hasn't put together the Eli-Charlie puzzle. Just as I open my mouth to fill him in, she grips my bicep and whispers, "Let's go to the other hut."

I crack my neck and nod. We don't bother to say goodnight.

Once inside, we take off our wet clothes and wrap wool blankets around our naked bodies. Then we slam down a couple of sandwiches, feed her dogs, and drink about a gallon of water.

Afterward, we huddle together next to the potbelly stove.

"It was over Thanksgiving," she says quietly. "I was lonely. It was a mistake. I don't have feelings for him."

"Have you told him that?"

"It's complicated."

I stand and wrap a blanket around my waist. "This isn't Facebook, Chicken. You don't get to use that bullshit status with me."

She rubs her eyes. "He handles all my operations. He's got my bank passwords, the keys to the agency, the access to our databases. I can't log in and change everything. I don't have a computer. I keep blowing him off. I don't know what else to do. This situation requires finesse, Elliott. I have to wait until we're out of here." She buries her face in her hands. "I'm exhausted. Can't we talk about this tomorrow?"

I help her up and shuffle her over to a bunk. We hold each other tight for a long while, until our tired muscles give out. "This isn't over." I tilt her chin up. "Just because we're off that mountain, doesn't mean everything goes back to the way it was."

A raspy sigh of relief follows. "Thank you. I needed to hear that."

"I can't make love to you," I say after a bit. "I'm too tired. Rain check?"

"Top or bottom?"

I grab her ass. "I love you on top."

"No, I mean the bed. Top or bottom bunk?"

"Bottom, I guess."

We tuck ourselves in, and just as I'm about to crash, she peeks over the edge and whispers, "I love you."

"Would it be weird if I wept like a child?"

She snorts. "A little."

"I feel like someone gave us a second chance. Like I need to seize life by the balls and do something amazing."

"Me, too. It's almost like I've just given birth…*to me*. Charlotte Sullivan, born again." She giggles and yawns.

"'Night, Chicken."

"'Night, Loser."

FORTY

Eli Is A Loser

ORION	SHIMURA
6	6

Survival Tip*: Decisions should be based on the information you've gathered, as well as the nature of the terrain.*

Eli's Mixtape: Kishi Bashi, "Can't Let Go, Juno"

THE NEXT MORNING, Burt and Art haul us out of the yurts on snowmobiles. Most everyone is in dire pain, due to hangovers.

Charlie and I are so banged up we can barely walk. Her godfathers do us a favor and take us back last, so we can soak our bruised and battered bodies in the hot springs.

I'm in pain, not just from the avalanche, but because the future has arrived.

Today's the last day of camp. Two days before Christmas Eve.

I don't think I've ever been less excited for the holidays. I know Charlie invited me to spend them with her, but I can't get over the feeling that the promises made on the mountain aren't to be taken seriously—those plans were made under duress.

Later, back at the lodge, everyone is in their rooms. The atmosphere is still and heavy and cramped, like the log walls are getting ready to fall in.

There's something uneasy between Charlie and I today. She's been super short with me. Not about anything in particular. It's the usual Sullivan stubborn stuff—asserting her independence, refusing help for the stupidest things. I think she expects the worst.

And then there's Alan. His blatant denial kills me. Is he blind or stupid or crazy or what? I don't get it.

I get that she doesn't want to rock the boat, but it's causing a rift between us. I know it's jealousy talking, but I guess I still don't trust her. What if something happens to us, and she turns to him?

It feels like I'm walking on unstable ground, like tremors are rocking the planet.

Do I go back to New York? Do I stay here? What do I do? How do I figure out the rest of my life in a few days?

Charlie and I haven't even had a chance to discuss what happens after this is over.

In the afternoon, I meditate in my room. That's the only thing I can think to do—clear my mind.

It doesn't work.

Instead, I ponder the pros and cons of giving up my life—my simple life—back in New York. At one point, I get so tired I give up and fall asleep.

Two hours later, I wake up to the smell of grilled meat and baked bread. Proton asked us to dress up for the awards ceremony dinner tonight. They've hired caterers, bartenders, and even a DJ for the party. I'm a little insulted they didn't ask me. But then again, they know nothing about my past life.

They're announcing the winner tonight. After the avalanche, Proton gave both teams a point. That means we're tied. Skip's been baked all day. The man's stressed beyond belief.

He's not the only one.

After I dress, I meet everyone in the dining hall. The table is crowded with food.

Charlie and I send clandestine glances to each other. She's not hiding behind a mask tonight. There is nothing but worry in those brown eyes.

Under the table, I hold her hand. Her palm is sweaty and cool. I grip hers tighter, not letting go.

Once dinner is over, we head to the den. Malcolm is the MC, and tonight, he's dressed in full drag. He makes dumb jokes, and while people laugh, I feel sick to my stomach. I want to beg him to slow down, not talk so fast, let the night linger as long as it can.

Staying true to the authenticity of a real camp, Proton hands out individual awards to everyone.

Orion is first onstage. Stanley receives an award for "Loudest Camper." In reality, he's the quietest guy I've ever met.

Deadhead Duffy gets "Best Hair."

Christian Christine receives "Most Likely To Be Picked up on Prostitution Charges."

Joy gets "The Most Positive Camper."

Wang receives "Biggest Slob."

"Most Sedate" goes to Charlie.

Big surprise, I get "Busiest Beaver."

Sam scores "Worst Dancer."

"Best Trash Talker" goes to Preeti.

Jerry gets "Classiest."

Avery, "Most Energetic."

Sabrina, "Most Likely to Solve World Hunger." She doesn't "get" her award.

The best award goes to Alan. "Human Vulture." "Not sure what that means," he says with a tight smile.

It means he's been pecking at my scraps the whole time.

Art tells him it's related to his voracious appetite, and then he asks Skip to come onstage.

Burt lays a hand on Skip's shoulder and steps up to the mic.

Holy shit! Maybe we will win this business after all. Shimura needs this so bad. I stand up and pace in the back of the theater.

"I'd just like to say what a pleasure it's been to have you all here," Burt says. "I realize you probably all feel like a bunch of guinea pigs, but you've helped us see some of the kinks we need to iron out when we open up for business."

Yeah, like not sending campers to their deaths.

"Before I hand out this next award," he continues. "I'd like to extend an offer to spend the holidays with us. This is the first time Art and I won't be traveling, and we're planning on making Christmas extra special here at the lodge. We're decorating a tree and having a big party, so if you don't have any plans, stay the weekend with us." He clears his throat. "All right, this last award is the only serious one of the bunch."

I stop pacing and straighten my spine. *Here it comes.*

"Skip, in you we saw a great leader—"

Someone in the crowd coughs a laugh.

Burt directs his speech to the audience. "A great leader is someone who can step back and delegate, who pushes his staff to do their best. Someone who can instill humor into a serious situation. And someone who sacrifices his own happiness, for the sake of his employees."

Everything the old man says is true. Skip's a shiny diamond disguised as sarcastic coal.

He didn't want to run his dad's agency. But he did it anyway, because he didn't want to let anyone down.

Burt hands the trophy to him. "Congratulations, Shimura,

you win the award for 'Most Likely to Succeed,' and we mean that, sincerely."

Skip's brows rise a foot. "Does that mean I won the business?"

"Ah, no." Burt says, unapologetically. "Orion won the business. But you've got a great future ahead of you, kid." He actually has the gall to slap him on the back.

Skip walks out and leaves the award on the podium.

The only sound in the room is Avery's heavy sigh.

The DJ dims the lights and blasts disco music over the speakers.

None of us have moved from our seats yet.

I feel Skip's disappointment deep in my gut. I wish there was something I could do for him.

A sort of hypnotic trance takes over my thoughts as I watch the disco light spin. I could quit. I could quit and move here and work with Charlie. That makes one less person he has to lay off. And I get to be with her.

Problem solved.

Then why can't I take in a full breath?

FORTY-ONE

Charlie Sleeps With A Boy

October 1998

I<small>T WAS</small> Elliott's thirteenth birthday last night. His mom and dad did something bad, so he spent it with us.

He was so mad that Weiner gave him an ax and let him hack down two of our trees. Dad almost had a coronary.

He won't tell me what happened, but I know it had something to do with catching his parents in the middle of some sort of kinky sex.

I overheard him telling Mom about it.

Later, I let him sneak into my bedroom and sleep with me. He smells like bubble gum, and his hair is so soft. Like feathers.

It may have been the worst birthday for him, but for me, it was the best day ever.

FORTY-TWO

Charlie Beats A Stoner

Eli's Mixtape: Snoop Dog, Whiz Khalifa (feat. Bruno Mars), "Young, Wild & Free"

THERE WAS NEVER any doubt I'd win the business, but I didn't expect to feel bad about it.

Elliott told me Skip will probably have to lay people off.

There's also the fact that I can't really guarantee my own staff's future once I sell the agency to Grayson Advertising.

I should feel like celebrating. Instead, I feel a foreboding sense of dread.

After the awards ceremony, I sneak outside to the hot tub, to gather my thoughts.

I find Skip there, smoking a joint and staring at the stars.

"Mind if I join you?"

He gestures a hand to the adjacent seat.

"Sorry, Skip. I know how much you need this business."

"Don't sweat it. I never expected to get it."

"Really? How come you didn't leave?"

"Because I'm having fun. This will probably shock the shit out of you, but I'm not much of a business-y kind of guy. If I didn't like money so much, I'd be content to spend my life surfing, boarding, and living in a van."

"But you like money."

He takes a hit off the joint and blows out a smoke-suffocated "Exactly." He rests the back of his head on the edge of the tub. "Maybe one of these days, I can do something like this. Make money off other people's vacations."

"My dad once said it was not a good idea to turn your passion into a job. It stops being fun."

"Makes sense."

The water foams and fizzes around our silence. "So…Eli tells me you have to let some people go."

He sinks lower under the water. "I don't know. I've been selling my personal stock, trying to keep the agency afloat, but at some point, I'm going to have to stop caring and start becoming a ruthless asshole."

"I hate firing people. It's the worst part of the job. I'm probably going to have to do that when I get back to real life."

"Let me guess—Alan?"

I nod.

"That guy kind of reminds me of a diluted Jerry Reno. There's something about him. I can't put my finger on it."

"I'm not a very good judge of character."

"I don't know about that. St. James is a pretty stellar guy." He offers me the last of his joint.

I turn it down.

"So are you going to steal away my designer?" he asks.

"I hope so. He's being wishy-washy."

"Can you blame him?"

"No."

"He's a smitten kitten."

"Think so?"

"I'm terrible at my own relationships, but when it comes to other people's, I'm like an old matchmaker."

I snicker.

"I can always see when something special is about to begin. Saw it with my best friend, when she and my art director took off on a business trip together. Saw it with her sister a year later when she met St. James's roommate. It's like watching the spark at the end of a dynamite fuse. They burn and chase each other until they explode." His hands burst out of the water in a mock explosion.

I smile. "I like that."

He flicks a finger. "Ah, but what happens after the fire burns out is the true test of love. So far, I haven't been wrong."

I can't imagine our fire ever dying. Ours has been burning for a decade.

Skip stretches his neck and sighs. "I think Avery, Sam, Preeti, and I are going to stay for Christmas. We're all orphans."

"I'd like that a lot, and I know Elliott would too." I pause. "I wish we could all have a happy ending."

"We'll be fine. I'll be fine. Eli can have his Buddhism bullshit. I've already found the trick to happiness."

"Weed?"

"A sense of humor. Don't take life too seriously. That's my motto."

I think about how intense my life has been. There hasn't been a lot of laughter over the years. Real laughter, anyway.

But I've been born again. And baby Charlotte just may tattoo Skip's words on her wrist as a reminder of that.

"I like you, Skip."

"I like you, too, Turkey."

"Chicken."

"Whatevs. Punch that button and get those bubbles fired up."

FORTY-THREE

Eli Soaks It In

Survival Tip: Do not panic if you are trapped. Panic causes people to do foolish things, which increases danger. Find shelter and wait until you're certain it's safe to move on.

Eli's Mixtape: Tame Impala, "Elephant"

WHEN THE AFTER-PARTY starts winding down, I head upstairs in search of Charlie, eager to get our own private awards ceremony underway. Instead, I find Alan coming out of her room.

"What are you doing?" I snap.

He flinches and spins around with his hands up. "Looking for Charlotte."

"No, really." I place my forearm on the wall above him. "What *are* you doing?"

A weasel-faced smile creeps up. "Guess the best man won," he says. "Or should I say the best woman?"

"Why were you in her room?"

"I know what you're doing with her," he snipes. "You're just some fly-by-night guy that's filling the holiday void she gets this time of year." He ducks out from under me. "But here's the thing—I live here. I work with her. I know her."

I step closer. "You're deranged, you know that? Keep away from her. She's not interested. Now run along."

He doesn't move. "She told me about you. A long time ago, when she was drunk. She doesn't need more heartbreak."

My head heats up to a thousand degrees. I cock back my fist, ready to strike.

"What's up, guys?" Charlie says, padding down the hallway in a swimsuit with a towel around her.

"Just coming to congratulate you. Great job, boss." Eyeing me at the same time, Alan kisses her cheek.

He's just dying for me to punch his face.

Her nervous laugh is back. "You too, Al." She pauses. "'Kay, well, I better get dressed."

Alan slinks down the stairs and crawls back inside his hole.

"I don't like that guy," I say. "He's bad news. Watch out for him."

She opens her door and drags me in. "He's harmless. Just be patient a little while longer." Her hand smooths back my hair. "Come snuggle with me."

The towel drops, as does her suit, and she takes a running leap into bed and buries herself under the covers.

Still jacked up on Alan rage, I lie on top and fold my hands across my chest.

Her nose peeks out. "Aren't you going to get in?"

"Not right now."

"I won," she says solemnly.

"You did."

"I talked to Skip. I think he'll be okay."

"Yeah, probably."

"What about us?"

I turn to my side and play with her hair. "I could come work with you?"

She frowns. "I'm selling the agency."

I jerk back. "What?"

She nods. "To Grayson. They want to buy me out."

"Let me get this straight, you went through all of this bullshit, so you could sell your business?" I rub my eyes. I can't believe it.

"It was the plan all along. I want to travel."

"Why didn't you tell me?"

"Because this is the first time you've given me any indication you're interested in a future."

I flop on my back and sigh. "Goddammit, Charlie, why do you have to be so difficult?"

She pops out from under the blankets, straddles my chest, and pins my arms over my head. She bites her way down my neck then licks my nipples and continues below. "You love me."

I hold back her hair so I can get a better view. "I do. I really, really do."

FORTY-FOUR

Eli Visits The Swingers

Survival Tip: *When you're on an adventure, sometimes it's important to realize how far you've come, not how far you have to go.*

Eli's Mixtape: Elbow, "Trust the Sun"

ON CHRISTMAS EVE MORNING, Charlie perches on top of me naked. "Merry Christmas, Loser."

I play with my fidget toys, her nipples. "Your bruises are almost gone," I tell her.

"Almost healed." She stretches and yawns, elongating her lean body.

"Is this my Christmas present? Waking up with you on top of me?" I grip her hips and grind my hard-on against her.

She moves back a little and plays with my cock, then rises and guides me into her. We don't move. I relish the feeling of our connection, warm and wet.

"I have a surprise for you," she says.

I slide in and out. "It's fantastic. Thank you."

She caresses her clit until I take over the duty. "Not now. Later."

"Mmm. I can't wait."

Three minutes post orgasm, Charlie lays beside me and drapes a long leg across my body. "I called your parents. We're going over there tonight for dinner."

Instantly, my dick shrinks and slips out of her. "You what?"

"They're expecting us at five."

I sit up. "I didn't tell you to do that."

"Elliott, your mom told me she hasn't seen you since you left. How could you be so cold? They're your parents. They love you."

"They're more interested in kinky sex than me."

She gives me an old witch eye. "You sound like Christine."

"Oh, yeah? Well, if you found your parents in the middle of an orgy on your thirteenth birthday, you wouldn't be so open-minded." I put furious finger quotes around open-minded.

"Is that what happened?"

Feeling exposed suddenly, I jump up and put on my pajama bottoms.

She takes my hand. "Sit down and talk to me."

I keep standing. "Remember that night I slept with you on my birthday?"

A big smile takes over her face. "I logged it in my journal as the best day of my life. Wonder what happened to that journal? Anyway, you and Weiner killed our trees."

"That was Patrick's idea. I needed to take my rage out on something. The point is, they don't care about me."

"That's not what your mom said. She cried when she heard you were in town and didn't call her."

I rub the ache out of my chest. "How are we going to get to Evergreen?"

"Burt said we could use the van."

I secretly pray for a blizzard. Unfortunately, the sky is so blue it hurts my eyes.

Later in the morning, us remaining campers pile in the van with Burt and Art to take Austin to see Santa and the chocolate village in Keystone. He screams bloody murder the minute he sees the jolly elf.

After that shitshow, we return to the lodge and go ice-skating. Then we drink hot chocolate in front of the fireplace and decorate an enormous tree.

Earlier, Burt and Art made us draw names out of a hat for secret Santa gifts. They're big on the spirit of the holidays, so they insisted everyone make gifts, instead of buying into the consumerism. That's exactly the sort of thing the filthy rich do.

I chose Skip. My gift to him is my salary. I'm fairly certain Avery and I are the highest-paid employees at Shimura. He could save two jobs just by losing me.

I still want to do something special for Charlie though. And if anything, visiting my parents tonight gives me an opportunity to do that.

At four o'clock, Charlie snags a bottle of wine from the cellar, and we bundle up and head out to the van.

❄

MY MOTHER IS STANDING in the yard crying when we arrive. I've talked to her on the phone over the years. She and Dad are on my Facebook, but this is the first time I've seen her in person in a decade.

I take after her Nordic roots. We're both tall and blond and thin. Our eyes are virtually the same color, although with age, hers have turned a lighter shade of blue.

My parents look like a stock photo that might come up in a search for "handsome retired couples." They still hike and play tennis and ride bikes and fuck other people.

My mom sees me hesitate and hugs Charlie before she hugs

me. "It's so good to see you. I've thought about you so much over the years."

"This place looks exactly the same," Charlie says inside our house. "You still have the same furniture."

It's like stepping into a museum exhibit of my childhood. It even smells the same, like mashed potatoes and my dad's aftershave.

I feel like a moody teenager all of a sudden, with an overwhelming need to run to my room and hide.

"Your father's watching *A Christmas Story* in the den," Mom titters. "Gary's in the kitchen. We're fixing the mash potatoes for dinner. Would you like some wine?"

I love how she breezed right over the Gary part. The part where there's another man living in the house and having a bisexual relationship with my parents.

Charlie shoots me a confused look. "Gary?"

I shake my head, warning her not to bring it up. I purposely hid that tidbit from her. Honestly, I didn't think he'd be here. The guy moved in a couple of years ago so he could screw my parents on a full-time basis.

"I'll be right out with the wine," my mom sings. "Go see your dad. He's so excited you could make it."

My father is not excited to see me. He doesn't even get up out his seat to greet us. "Hey," he says, keeping his attention on *A Christmas Story*. "Your favorite show's on. It's almost at the naked leg lamp part."

Charlie and I take a seat and watch the scene unfold.

"It's indescribably beautiful!" Ralphie's dad cries.

"The soft glow of electric sex gleaming in the window."

"It reminds me of the Fourth of July! You should see what it looks like from out here."

I study my dad as he regards the TV, his hair now completely gray, his mouth tilted up in an amused half-smile, and this sensation sweeps through me, like I'm watching a movie of my life—*The St. James' Dysfunctional Christmas.*

"I'm going to see if your mom needs help," Charlie says.

After she's gone, I carry on staring at my father, trying to figure out how this man contributed to my DNA. We don't look alike. Our personalities are completely different. And there's the part where he swings both ways and gets off on group sex.

We have nothing in common, except a fondness for this movie. For a second, I wonder if this man is even my father.

"Can I ask you something, Dad?"

He mutes the program. "Shoot."

"What's it like fucking other people when you're married to Mom?"

My dad swivels his recliner so he's facing me and blows out a harsh sigh. "You know, son, I can't tell you how pleased I am that these are the first words out of your mouth to me in a decade." The frown on his face tells an epic story of disappointment.

"Since we're not bothering with the social pleasantries," my dad says, "I'll just jump right in and say what's on my mind. Your mother and I have gone through many cycles over the years with our relationship. You didn't want much to do with us. You were always over at the Sullivans' house. She felt a void. I think a lot of women go through that, when their kids grow up."

He studies me for a second before he continues. "At the same time, I was trying to make partner at the law firm. I could barely make it home to give her a kiss goodnight. Your mother's always been a very sexual person. We agreed she could play with other men, as long as nothing came out of it. We've always been adventurous with our sex life, and I never had a problem with it. Neither did she."

"And what about the time I found you on my birthday?"

"Well, we were experimenting with ecstasy that day. Things got out of control. I'm not proud of it. But the thing is, and maybe you'll learn this one day if you ever decide to have children, just because you have kids doesn't mean you're a grown-up. Marriage is far more complicated than a TV show, and it pisses me off when people try to dictate the rules. Particularly you, the son who hasn't graced us with his presence in ten years."

"And that guy in the kitchen?" I point my chin. "What about him?"

"Gary? We have a lot of fun together. And bottom line? We're not hurting anyone."

It's hurting me. But this is ten-year-old me—the Ralphie who wants his holidays to be like a Fifties' Christmas, with a mom and dad who'd rather embarrass me with a bunny suit than a bisexual relationship.

For a minute, I put aside my childhood and study my father. I look at him as if he were a man and not a parent. I feel sorry for him. And I feel sorry for me.

"So you're back with Charlie?" he asks after a long silence.

I nod.

"What's she been up to? Your mother said you were out here on business?"

I nod again.

Dad scratches his stubble then releases a shaky breath. His mouth quivers, and his eyes redden.

I've never seen my dad cry before. I cover my face to hide my own tears.

He gets up and hugs me.

It's incredibly awkward.

"I've missed you, son. I've missed you since you were a little kid running around with Patrick and didn't want to hang out with us anymore." He yanks out a tissue from a box on the side table and honks into it. "We can't change the past. But we can change the future."

I glom onto that line, because it's sort of the theme of my life at the moment.

"Let's go see what Mom's making," he says.

Right then, I feel this expansiveness, like I'm finally free. I've finally let go of all the guilt and shame and pain of my past, and I can grow up and be an adult.

Except, there's still a twinge of tightness that keeps me from being completely at peace—fear of the unknown.

I wish I had my fucking quote-of-the-day app. Burt still hasn't given me back my phone.

During dinner, Charlie keeps things light and airy and small-talk-y. She's doing this as a favor to me, because she can tell I'm at a loss for words.

Every time there's a pause, my mom asks me a question about our relationship. I think she has her mind set on grandkids.

Can you imagine Gary in that scenario? How would I explain that to my kids?

Wait, am I thinking about having children with Charlie? The room spins for a minute as I process this thought.

I suddenly can't picture my life without her in it.

When the meal is over, no one lingers around the table. Gary and my Dad jet to the den to watch TV. Charlie and I do the dishes. My mom packs up the leftovers. And then it's time to head back.

Just before we leave, I sneak off to my old room. It shocks me to find it in the same condition I left it.

My snowboard trophies line the shelves. Posters of Nineties' grunge metal bands still cover the walls. My clothes are still hanging in the closet.

Mom comes in and sits on my bed. "Can I help you find something?"

"Why did you keep all this?"

She fiddles with the buttons on her Christmas blouse for a second. "I don't know. Seems silly, I guess, but when you left, part of me thought you'd come back. Moms have a hard time letting go of their babies."

A memory of her dropping me off at the airport appears

through the fog—her begging me not to leave, telling me to heal my leg and talk to Charlie before I made a huge mistake.

I should have listened to her.

I open the top drawer of my dresser. Inside is the bag I was hoping to find. I stuff it in my pocket and grab a framed picture off one of my shelves and zip it inside my coat.

"Are you coming back this time?" my mom asks.

I close my eyes and stop breathing, willing the answer to come. "I don't know, yet."

"I've always secretly hoped you two would get back together."

Me too, I think, but I don't say it, because this is too much right now. I'm not built for this. I can only handle so much drama at one time.

She rises from the bed and hugs me tight. "Please call me the instant you get back to the lodge. Or I'll stay up all night worrying."

The back of my throat narrows. My mom still worries about me after I've been such an ungrateful son. How is that possible? How can you love someone after they've been such a dick?

When we say our goodbyes, my parents cry. I try not to. Then we start up the van and head back to Breckenridge.

Not even halfway down our driveway, Charlie says, "Well? Are you glad I made you go?"

"Yeah," I say and leave it at that.

"You're such a man." She snorts and stuffs her hand in my pocket. "What's this?" She pulls out the bag I put in there it earlier.

"Don't!" I swerve and correct the van just before I bash into a stop sign.

It's too late. She's already opened the box. Her hand flies to her mouth. "Is this—?"

"I bought it a long time ago."

"It's…" She turns to me with mirth in her eyes. "Hideous. Oh my God."

I wince. "It was the style back then."

"Jesus, what were you thinking?" She picks up the ring and examines it in the light, looking as if she might vomit. "I thought you knew me."

"I should have asked you to pick it out. I'm not good at those things. You know that."

She snaps it back inside the box and stares out the window.

"Chicken?"

She doesn't answer. A car honks behind me, and I shift the van into gear.

"Are you mad?"

"You had it engraved."

"I did."

"'Mine, all mine.'"

I chuckle. "I was kind of a dick back then."

She faces me, looking hollowed out. "Why didn't you propose?"

"I was going to. But then your parents…" I can't finish the sentence.

Her gaze shifts back to the window, but her fingers reach for mine.

I bring our clasped hands to my lap.

"What are you going to do with that ring?" she asks.

It comes charging back—the tightness in my chest. I don't answer her, because, truthfully, I'm not sure what I'm doing with it. "It's sort of a moot point now."

She turns on the heat. The windows fog up, and she draws a heart on hers then wipes it off.

On the way back, she falls asleep, and we don't bring up the ring again.

FORTY-FIVE

Charlie Finds A Treasure

October 2005

WEINER FOUND Elliott's engagement ring. Squee! I wonder when he's going to propose? I'm so in love and so happy.

December 2005

It's been two months, and that ring is still not mine. I'm pissed. So are mom and dad. What the hell is taking so long?

FORTY-SIX

Charlotte Makes Love

Eli's Mixtape: She & Him, "All I Want For Christmas is You"

ON CHRISTMAS MORNING, I let Elliott make love to me—a gift for both of us.

I shed a few tears when it's over. It's been so long since I've experienced this kind of intimacy. I'm scared of the way it makes me feel. Especially because it doesn't seem like he's made up his mind about us.

Afterward, he wipes my tears and kisses me. Then he gives me his gift.

It's an old framed picture of the three of us. In the photo, Patrick and I are wearing these dumb hats my mom knitted us. Elliott is wearing a puffy coat three times too big for him. My old dog, Sir-Farts-A-Lot, is in the picture, and we all have plastic sleds.

I rub my cheek against his soft beard. "I love it."

"That's not all," he says. "I made you a mixtape."

"A real mixtape?"

"No, online. Malcolm let me borrow his laptop last night."

"Yay! I can't wait to listen to it."

"My turn!" I jump off his lap and pull a box out from under the bed.

His brow lifts. "Beaver wrapping paper? Did Burt buy this?"

I bounce on the bed. "Open it!"

He tears off the paper and holds up the Ken doll glued to a tongue depressor. "World's Greatest Lover?" He turns to me. "Is this supposed to be me?"

"The stick's supposed to be a snowboard. Maybe you didn't win the race, but you still deserve a major award."

"I see. Why am I wearing bedazzled feather underwear?"

"That was the only craft supplies here."

The St. James smirk shows up. "This is better than winning a gold medal at the Olympics."

I kiss him hard. "I knew you'd love it."

Downstairs people are stirring. "Let's go see what Austin does when he sees all those presents under the tree."

We dress in our tacky Christmas sweaters and make our way to the den. Burt's building a fire, and Christmas songs play softly in the background.

Avery is on the floor with her little boy, watching his frenzied excitement. "Santa came! Mommy! Santa came."

"I told you the fire wouldn't hurt him." She winks at me. There's a huge smile on her face. I imagine it has something to do with seeing her son so delighted.

Maybe one day, I'll get to see my own child light up like that.

Art heads to the kitchen, and soon, the scent of fresh orange juice, coffee cake, bacon, cinnamon, and mulled wine warm the lodge.

Sam arrives at breakfast. "Morning everyone."

Eli nods. "Fischer."

Preeti floats into the dining hall with her hair tumbling down her back in black waves. She's wearing a bright red sari.

It's like a flashbulb goes off and lights Skip up. In an instant, his expression returns to smugly bored.

Malcolm toddles out, wearing striped adult-sized footie pajamas. "Oh my gawd, I'm starving."

"Eat up," Burt says. "You're doing the dishes."

"Nun-uh. I'm off today."

"Guess I'll take back that holiday overtime."

"Christ, old man. Least let me eat some Danish before you beat me."

He's such a drama queen.

My smile is big, and my laughter is real. And as I look around the table, I see family. Not my original family. My new family. My tribe. Eli, his lovely friends, my crazy godfathers. Even Malcolm.

I don't know why I avoided coming up here for so long. I guess I thought it would make me feel empty. But it doesn't.

I feel whole again.

FORTY-SEVEN

Eli Has A Merry Christmas

Survival Tip: The warmth and comfort of a fire is a great morale booster.

Eli's Mixtape John Lennon, The Plastic Ono Band, The Harlem Community Choir, "Happy Xmas (War is Over)"

I DON'T THINK I've ever enjoyed Christmas until today. The last few years, I've spent the holidays with my roommate Elias and his band over at his mom Annie's house. She's Chinese, so most of the time we end up at a dim sum restaurant in the afternoon, and that's that.

It's different today. The holiday spirit glows inside me. It's as toasty as the fire and as radiant as the woman next to me. It doesn't feel real.

Seeing all of us gathered around a ginormous tree, opening gifts and drinking mulled wine, while Art bellows out Frank Sinatra and Avery's little boy bounces with joy—it's like taking a walk in the snow and peering through someone else's windows.

Even Skip is smiling. And it's not creepy. He just gave Preeti her gift.

The intern folds back tissue from the tiny box and holds up a red origami butterfly. "It's…wow. Did you make this?"

Skip sits back and loses the grin. "You don't like it?"

"No, it's beautiful." She sets it back in the box and lifts an astonished gaze back to my boss. "I had no idea you were so talented."

Skip rubs his hands. "Who's next?"

"Me," Sam says. "I picked little man." He disappears for an instant and comes back with a life-size gorilla and Santa-sized bag of presents.

"Sam!" Avery covers her mouth. "What in the world?"

Austin tackles the gorilla.

Sam chuckles and high-fives the kid.

Avery shakes her head.

"Oh, come on," Sam says. "I'm not going to make a kid a present. It's Christmas."

"Don't you think you went a little overboard? How am I going to get all that home?"

"I'll ship it." He hands another gift to the kid, who tears through it and tosses it in a pile.

"Say thank you, Austin," Avery tells him, shaking her head at Sam.

He tears into another package. "Tank you, Austin."

Charlie leans over and whispers in my ear. "I think Sam has a crush on Avery."

I tilt my head and study the two. "I don't see it."

She shakes her head. "Men are so dumb."

Avery retrieves a package under the tree and hands it to Sam. "I drew you."

He shakes the gift in front of Austin. "What do you think it is, buddy? A ray gun?"

"It's a book," the kid says.

Sam chuckles and unwraps the book. It's a tattered copy of *The Princess Bride*, by William Goldman.

"I brought it with me from home. It's my favorite book," she said. "I noticed you like to read."

"I do." He has a big ole goofy grin. "And I love the movie. 'When I was your age, television was called books.'" He ruffles Austin's hair. "Your mom's a pretty cool lady."

Avery hides her smile behind her mug of wine.

"Want to be my daddy?" Austin asks.

She chokes, and I get hit in the face with her wine spray.

Sam cracks up. "Think you freaked out your mom there, kiddo."

"Austin, we don't say that to people."

"That's okay. I'm flattered. Not every day a kid asks you to be their dad." He laughs again then buries his nose in the book.

Charlie pinches my thigh and gives me a bouncy brow look.

It's my turn. The envelope with my resignation burns a hole in my back pocket. This doesn't feel like the right time. Not with everyone here. "I drew you, Skip. But I'm going to give you my gift later."

My boss cups an ear. "I keep hearing echoes of Jerry Reno, shouting, 'That's what she said.'"

Everyone laughs.

Malcolm gives Charlie an old hoodie with the word *Bitch* bedazzled on the back.

"This is the best gift ever." She puts it on and models it for us.

Art passes Avery an envelope. "Little something for Austin's college fund. Don't open it now."

"Really? You didn't have to do that."

"We enjoyed having him around."

Avery tears up. "This is the best Christmas I've ever had."

"Here! Here!" I say, and we all clink mugs.

Austin gives Burt a new pair of bunny slippers, made out of leftover pink feathers and socks.

Field-Tripped • 229

Preeti gifts Malcolm a watercolor painting she made of the mountains.

Burt gives me the same GPS tracker we lost in the avalanche. "Maybe you can find your way to the sink and shave that fuzz off your face."

I ignore the beard comment. "I'll cherish it. Thank you."

Once all the gifts are handed out, we set up everything for the party. At four o'clock, Burt and Art's friends arrive—an uproarious and diverse community.

There's singing and dancing and games. The food and drink overfloweth.

Charlie and I sneak away periodically to make out in dark corners. "This is the best Christmas I've had in years."

"Me, too," I say and tweak her nipples.

Around ten, all of the guests leave, and while Charlie helps clean up, Skip calls for a Shimura team huddle in his private hot tub.

It's only big enough for four people, but five of us cram in and pass around a bottle of peppermint schnapps.

"I'm pissed you got this room and not me," I tell him.

"I have a hot tub," Avery tells me.

"Me, too," Sam says.

I glance at Preeti. She shrugs.

"So I'm the only one without a private hot tub?"

"I don't think your woman has one, does she?" Sam asks.

"I think we all know the answer to that," Avery says.

Everyone fists-bumps her except me.

"So what are you going to do now?" she asks. "You're going back to New York, right?"

I rub the back of my neck. "Actually, I was thinking about resigning. That was the gift to Skip I was talking about earlier."

It's quiet except for the sound of the jets splashing water over the sides.

"Sure you want to do that?" Skip asks.

I stare up at the moon. "Honestly? No. But I love her. I always have. It's a lot to take in, in a short amount of time."

"I don't blame you one bit," Avery says. "I will never give up my life for a relationship again. I can't tell you how many times I've had to reinvent myself for a man. It's not worth it."

Sam's brows knit. "Who said he has to give up his life? Maybe you've had some bad luck, but that doesn't mean all relationships are like that."

"Did she ask you to give up your job?" Preeti asks.

"No, this is my idea."

Sam gestures to Avery. "See? He wants to do this. It's called sacrifice. People who love each other do that."

"I'm not sure it's really a sacrifice," I say.

"Are you saying my agency sucks, St. James?"

I chuckle. "Not at all. I love it there. And I love you guys."

"Aw, I love you, too," Avery says. "I'll miss you if you leave."

The conversation turns into this drunken I-love-you bonding moment, and we rehash memories of our crazy trip even though we're still here.

"We need to do this again," Sam says. "I had a blast."

Everyone takes a pull off the schnapps.

"This is so cliché," Avery says, "but it made me feel like a kid again. And Austin had a ball. Except for the spanking." She lowers her head in shame.

"He's not going to remember that, Avery," I tell her.

"I hope not."

"So what are you going to do about your ticket home tomorrow, St. James?" Skip asks. "Because, if you need a little more time, you can push the date. I booked them like that in case this turned out to be bullshit, which it was, but we had fun, and now I have to lay a bunch of people off."

"What was the question?" I ask.

"Are you coming back with us tomorrow?" Preeti asks.

I drag my hands down my face. "I don't know yet."

Sam shakes his head. "Dude. You better make up your mind. Second chances don't come around very often."

"Fuck. I know."

He shoves my shoulder. "Get out of here, and go talk to your lady."

I do exactly that. I dry off, find Charlie, and drag her to my room.

We snuggle in bed and recount the day's events like we're a real couple. And then at midnight, the grandfather clock downstairs gongs, and Christmas disappears.

"My plane back to New York leaves tomorrow night," I say, and as the words leave my mouth my chest caves in.

Her body tenses next to mine. "Don't go."

"Chicken."

She sits up. "I'm serious. You said you don't like your apartment, and you don't have any furniture. Quit your job. Stay."

"You said you were going to travel."

"Come with me."

"What am I going to do for money?"

"Burt and Art said we could help them with the camp."

"You asked them about me?"

"Does that bother you?"

"No, it's just..." *I'm not ready yet.*

Snow piles on the skylight above, and I feel like I'm under the avalanche again. *Thump. Thump. Thump. Thump.* My heartbeat is the only sound in the room.

This is such a big decision. I spent ten years trying to get over her. What if something bad happens again?

She threads her fingers through my hair. "I would tell you to take your time, but we've wasted enough time."

"Are you saying, if I leave, that's it? We're done?"

"I'm saying, it's time for me to start living again. I don't want to wait around for you anymore."

"That feels like an ultimatum."

"I want to be with you. I know what I want. And I'm sad that you don't."

"I want you," I tell her.

"But?"

I stroke her pretty face then turn back to the skylight. "About six months ago, I had a nervous breakdown. I threw my coffee at a barista."

"No way."

"He wrote 'feline' on my cup instead of 'Eli.' I was working all the time, not sleeping, dealing with tons of stress. I didn't hurt the guy, but I wanted to."

"I can't imagine you doing that."

"Yeah, well. That's the point. I sort of lost myself there for a minute. Crazy enough, a Buddhist monk was there when it happened. He gave me a card and told me to give him a call if I wanted to chat."

Her eyes widen. "A monk had a business card? What did it say?"

"It was the address of his temple. I went to see him later that afternoon. We talked, and he gave me some books. He told me about the eight-step path to happiness. After that, I started meditating, took a few classes. Then my roommate asked me to move out, and I decided it was time to make a change. Tried celibacy, vegetarianism."

She snorts. "How'd that work out for you?"

"Well, that's the other thing. I'm obviously not sticking with it."

"And that worries you?"

"We're different people now. We don't know each other." *What if I give up my life, and we're not compatible? What if I lose you again?*

"This is a big risk," she says softly. "For both of us. I may be channeling my inner-Christine here, but we both have to take a leap of faith and trust that this will work out. I love you. I've always loved you. I know in my heart you're the one for me."

I turn to her and kiss her softly. "You're the one for me, too. But if I get attached, I don't think I can survive losing you again."

"I can't survive if you leave." She flicks off the lamp and pulls my arms around her. "Let's talk about it in the morning."

I watch her face in the moonlight. Her eyes close, and her lips pop open. When we were dating, I used to hear that little pop and know she was out.

I want to hear that every night.

FORTY-EIGHT

Eli Gets Knocked Down

Survival Tip*: Earthquakes are caused by the sudden release of built-up tension. They are perhaps the most feared of all nature's violence, because they arrive suddenly and with little warning. If you survive, brace yourself for aftershocks.*

Eli's Mixtape: M. Ward, "Clean Slate"

EARLY THE NEXT MORNING, my coworkers pack up to leave. The finality of it settles in my stomach.

Skip pulls me aside. "So what'd you decide? Do I need to find a new designer?"

I scratch my beard. "Is it okay if I give you my answer later? I changed my flight so I could have more time."

"Your job may still be there, but your woman won't be." He sighs and places a hand on my shoulder. "I'm halfway tempted to fire you, to make it easy on you."

He removes his hand and pulls a joint out of his backpack. "You look stressed, St. James. So, I'm going to leave this with you. It's a crying shame I can't take it with me." He gives the joint a kiss and leaves it on the dresser.

I chuckle. "You're one of a kind, man. Best boss I've ever had."

"Good. You're talking in the past tense." He ushers me to the door. "All right, get out of here. I hate goodbyes. They make me tear up." He doesn't look the slightest bit emotional.

A little later, everyone piles in the van with Malcolm for the airport.

My body is twitching for a release, so I convince Charlie to go snowboarding.

On the mountain, it's sunny and sixty-five degrees. Colorado is tempting me back home with this gorgeous weather.

When we're on the chairlift, swinging high above the earth, Charlie asks, "What now?"

I don't answer her. Instead, I ride to the top in silence then jump off and race down the slopes.

Fear chases me, but it can't keep up. Neither can Charlie.

Endorphins pump through me. The feeling is like endless laughter.

I need this in my life. All of this. The challenge. The thrill. I can't give this up again. I can't give her up again.

At the bottom, she arrives ten minutes after me, panting.

"Did you time yourself? I bet that was fast enough to qualify for the Olympics." A ray of sun hits her face just right and lights up her smile.

"Let's do this," I say. "You and me? Let's do this."

She tackles me to the ground.

We laugh and hold onto each other. "I love you!" I shout.

"And I love you!" she shouts.

The world mills around us, happy conversation buzzing, bright cheeks glowing, people stumbling through the snow in heavy boots. But we don't move, because it's just she and I in this mad world and no one else.

And this moment? I let it sink deep into my long-term memory bank, to take out when we're old and riding around on scooters, probably racing each other around the grocery store aisles.

※

THAT AFTERNOON, we make love, and then we hold hands in bed and regard the intense blue through the skylight and start to make plans. We come up with these grand schemes.

"Let's go to Tibet," I say.

"I want to go fishing in Alaska and then see the northern lights."

"I want to record world music."

"Let's sit in cafes and talk about life with strangers."

We keep going like this, not letting the looming rain clouds dissolve our dreams. Money, our jobs, her dogs, our lives—we don't talk about those things.

I lie on my side and caress her naked splendor.

When she gets up to go to the bathroom, I see it—the bottle of medication on her nightstand. I pick it up and read the label.

She comes out a minute later and stops in her tracks.

"What's this for?" I ask.

"I...uh." She sits on the bed with her back facing me. "I've been depressed."

This jars me, but I don't let her see that. "Why? Because of the accident?"

"I don't know. I just am." Her voice is shaky.

"*Am?* You're still depressed?"

She turns to me. "I'm better. With you. But I can't just stop taking it."

I turn and stare out the skylight.

"I'm not perfect, Elliott," she says. "I've made a lot of mistakes over the years. Ideally this stuff would come up over time. But we haven't really had a chance to date."

"What else do I need to know?"

She sucks in a breath and then lets it out all at once. "I may or may not be a sex addict."

A laugh surges up from deep in my belly. "I can live with that."

"I'm serious. I'm not proud of it. I've been with a lot of men." Her knuckles are white from gripping the blanket.

"My roster is pretty lengthy as well," I say. "Happens when you've spent most of your life single."

This doesn't seem to cheer her up. "I just want you to know I'm not going to cheat on you."

My heart is racing. I believe her. And that scares me. "Okay."

And then, *bam!* An explosion. A knock on the door.

We don't move.

"Charlotte? It's Alan. Burt said you were up here. I thought with the DUI, you might need a ride home."

Bliss drains from my body like a slow leak in a balloon.

She jumps up from the bed and puts on her robe.

"Don't answer that door."

She ignores me. "I'll tell him to wait for me downstairs. I need to put an end to this."

"No, *I'll* tell him." I grab the blanket off the bed, wrap it around my waist, and swing open the door. "You just don't give up, do you?"

His mouth drops open then shuts tight. "You're still here."

I point down the hall. "Go downstairs, you fucking creep, before I beat your ass."

Charlie calls out behind me. "Alan, just go. I'll be down in a minute. We need to talk."

I slam the door in his face and don't turn around.

"I got a DUI a couple of months ago," she says.

I cringe like I just received a blow to the head.

"I'm not an alcoholic," she says. "I just made a bad happy hour decision. Nobody got hurt. I told you, I'm not perfect."

I rest my forehead against the door. "Fuck, Charlie. What else are you going to spring on me?"

"Look at me."

I turn and face her. I've never seen her look so fragile.

"Let me get rid of Alan first," she says. "Then we can finish our talk." She dresses in a hurry and leaves me in her room.

Her dogs stare at me, panting, waiting for me to make a move.

"I'm too attached," I say to them.

I give her twenty minutes. Then I get up and pack my things.

When I'm done, I head downstairs and wait. The grandfather clock ticks in the den, and when the second hand reaches the hour, it gongs six times.

Alan comes out of the game room without her. There's defiance on his face.

My pulse kicks up.

He stops and stands in front of me. "Cocky son of a bitch. Think you've won?" He grits his teeth and spits out more venom. "You have any idea how many men that whore has slept with? Besides you and me? Hundreds. And that's just since I've known her. I've done everything for that woman. I built her fucking business. And how does she repay me? With two weeks notice." He scoffs. "With her, you can't win. You'll end up losing, just like me."

Stomp! Stomp! Slam. He leaves like a violent tornado, annihilating everything in his path.

A minute later, she comes out and glances down at my backpack. "What are you doing?"

"I have to go."

Her spirit seems to wither. "Is this about Alan? I told him everything. I gave him two weeks. Did he tell you? What happened? Is he still here? What did he say to you? Why are you doing this? Everything is fine. It's over. Talk to me—"

"This is about me." My voice is wobbly, unsure. "I need time. To think. By myself. This is too much."

Her lips tremble and her eyes fill with tears. "You're panicking."

I hang my head. "You're like an earthquake, Charlie. Just when I think I know you, you shift and change. Then I have to start all over and learn a new route. It's what I love about you, but it's also what scares me the most."

"You think I'm not capable of stability? I've run a successful business for the last five years."

"No, that's not it. This isn't about you. It's about me."

She scoffs.

I grab her chin. "I'm not like you. I can't just make a spur of the moment decision. I need time to adjust. I need time to breathe. Let me do this. Please, give me some time, Chicken."

She bursts into tears. "You're the fucking chicken, not me."

FORTY-NINE

Charlie Loves Eli

December 2005

I WAS HANGING out with Mom and Dad today, and they asked me when I thought that Loser was going to propose. I told them I thought he'd probably do it after the Olympics. We have plenty of time. The rest of our lives.

FIFTY

Charlie Survives A Disaster

Eli's Mixtape: The Flaming Lips, "Do You Realize??"

ON THE DAY my family died, Elliott left me at the apartment to go identify their bodies.

The only thing I could think to do was take a hot bath. It seems so absurd now, but when I got that call from the police, it was like all the blood drained out of my body. I couldn't get warm enough. Scalding water seemed like the only cure.

When he came back, I took one look at his face and crumpled to the floor.

I don't ever want to see that look again.

He picked me up off the floor and tucked me in bed and didn't let go of me for the rest of the night. It was his arms that kept me together. If he wasn't there, I would have broken into a million tiny pieces.

The next week went by—the funeral, the unscented smell of wreaths, the casseroles, the *if-there's-anything-we-can-do's*—and he was by my side the entire time.

"I'll be okay," I remember thinking. *"As long as he's here, I'll be fine."*

Once the prayers and the dumb poetry and the pitiful looks disappeared, so did he.

I waited and waited and waited and let life pile up around me.

A week later, I took another hot bath. Then I drank a fifth of vodka and went out and danced with my old college roommate.

That night, I acted like nothing happened, because to me, nothing *had* happened. I'd already switched off the part of my brain that was willing to accept reality.

He came back the next morning and found me in bed with someone else.

I was in so much pain when he walked in, I completely forgot about the guy I picked up that night.

The way he stared through me—it was like I was a ghost.

It wasn't until six months later that I became aware of my loss. Before that, I'd been performing these rote tasks every day—getting out of bed, getting dressed, showering, walking to school—I don't know how I did it.

It was a trivial thing that triggered it. My license plate renewal arrived in the mail. Dad always handled that stuff for me.

Without even thinking, I called the house for him. The answering machine came on. "You've reached the Sullivans. We're not here. Please leave a message."

We're not here.

I didn't get out of bed for a month.

The phrase I hate most is "life goes on." For the last ten years, everyone's life has gone on but mine.

And now, after my world just started to spin again, it stops.

It's not fair. *It's my turn for a goddamned happy ending.*

I jam my palms against my eye sockets, hard enough to push my eyeballs to the back of my head.

I have to let him go. He needs me to let him go. That's the only way he'll come back.

Why can't I get past the feeling that this is it?

He crushes me in a hug that breaks my bones and leaves me limp. "I'll call you when I land."

"I'm not waiting, Elliott. Not this time. It's time to start living again. And if I have to, I'll do it without you."

FIFTY-ONE

Eli Gets His Head Out Of His Ass

Survival Tip: *Before abandoning camp, leave signs for the rescue party that you've been there and have moved on.*

Eli's Mixtape: Black Lips, "Can't Hold On"

IN THE VAN on the way to Denver, Burt glares at me in the rearview mirror. He doesn't turn on the radio. There's no chit chat, no ass chewing, no nothing.

I keep waiting for him to light into me. But he never does.

So I stare out the window at the passing scenery and ask myself the same question over and over. *What the fuck am I doing?*

When we get to the airport, instead of dropping me off, he parks and gets out.

"Where are you going?"

"You've got a couple hours." He jangles his keys and stuffs them in his pocket. "Might as well have a burger and a beer while I'm here. It's a long drive back."

"You don't have a ticket. How will you get past security?"

"I'll buy one."

I drop my bags on the curb. "Just say what you've got to say, Burt."

"Step aside, Beaver, I'm getting me a beer."

I check in and don't bother to ask where Burt plans on *not* going with his ticket.

He goes through security with me, gets his pocketknife taken away, acts like it's no big deal, and then asks me if I'm okay with watching the Broncos game.

I don't bother to answer him. I want him to go away. This intimidation strategy will not work.

We end up in a sports bar not too far from my gate. He orders a plate of fried jalapeño poppers, a well-done burger, and a beer. He finishes the beer and the burger, wipes his mouth, picks his teeth with a toothpick, and then speaks to me while focused on the football game.

"Alan's been after her for a while. Charlotte never seemed interested, so Mother Art never bothered to interfere. Never cared for him much."

I huff. "I'm guessing you don't like me much either."

"I'm still formulating an opinion. I will say this, though, you keep a level head."

"A level head," I repeat. This guy needs help. *I* need help.

"I was a drill sergeant in the Marines."

"Gee, you're kidding. I never would have guessed."

"Met Charlie's dad and Art over in Vietnam. Used to train young boys to die. But that's another story." He grabs a popper off the plate and chews it for an insufferably long time.

"In a lot of ways," he continues, "boot camp's like what you see in the movies. The yelling. The bullying. That's by design. It's about creating a hostile environment and teaching soldiers not to react to it."

"Is this about the name calling?" I ask.

He chuckles. "You never got angry."

"The hell I didn't."

"Well, you didn't show it. Not once did you lose your cool."

"I'm losing my shit right now."

"I'm aware of that."

I feel the need to defend myself. "Burt, she's been back in my life for less than two weeks. And it's been insanity every single second—avalanches, dog stranglings, Alan stalkings, Sabrina strippings—it's a lot."

"Yeah, well, Art cooked this whole thing up. Blame him, not me."

Slowly, I set down my beer. "What did you just say?"

"He saw your picture in *Rolling Stone*. You were at an advertising award show with your rock star buddy, El Love, or whatever his name is."

"I was in Rolling Stone?"

"The article was about your friend, but you were in the picture." He burps and pounds his chest. "When Charlotte's family died, and you left, she sort of went into a coma. All she did was talk about you. Your name was drilled into our heads. We got so sick of hearing about you. When we saw your name, it just clicked."

I'm still stuck on the previous part. "You made this whole thing up? You brought us out here because you thought it would be cute to get us back together?"

"Not entirely. We really were looking for an agency. Charlie wants to sell her business, and we're not crazy about Grayson. We tried to buy her out, but she's too stubborn, told us she's not our orphan charity case. But her team is better suited for the work. That said, I like Skip a lot. He reminds me of a buddy I had in Nam. Real sarcastic like him. Anyway, we've got some side ventures we're floating by Skip. That ought to keep him from closing his doors for a while."

Burt's not picking up on my disgust. "You know what? You guys are assholes."

"Maybe," he says. "But did you have fun?"

"What?"

"Did you have fun? Everyone else did. You guys were like a bunch of kids out there. Hell, it was worth it, messing with you, just to see Charlie come back to life. She's been walking around for ten years with that crazy fake smile."

"I hate that smile."

"She's smiling for real now. Until you left."

I drop my forehead in my hand and squeeze. I can't sort through this blizzard of information. It's too hard.

Burt slides a credit card to the bartender. "It's not easy risking everything for love," he says solemnly. "I get why you're leaving. Did the same thing when I left my wife and kids for Art. He didn't get that I needed time away from the relationship to figure things out. When I came back, he didn't want me. I was so pissed."

I slump over and sigh.

The bartender comes back, and Burt scrawls his signature on the bill. Then he unzips his jacket and slaps a gift with beaver wrapping paper on the bar.

"I was going to give this to Charlie on Christmas, but I ended up drawing your name for the Secret Santa. Found it in her parents' garage when Art and I cleaned it out. A little light reading for the flight home." He claps a hand on my shoulder and then heads out. "Merry Christmas."

I don't even want to know what it is. I stuff the gift in my bag and take out my phone. When I turn it on, a flurry of messages makes it vibrate non stop.

I search through all four hundred of them for one from Charlie. Not surprisingly, I don't find one.

But I *do* find ten calls from Elias, my old roommate. This worries me, since he never calls. He's much more of a text-only kind of guy. I ring him, and he answers right away.

"Puto, where have you been?" he asks.

"Colorado."

"Ah! We tried to invite you over for Christmas, but you never answered. We have an announcement."

"You're getting married," I say, suddenly regretting this call.

"Will you be my best man, dickhead?"

I sigh. "I guess."

Dead air.

"Still there?" he asks.

"Are you nervous? About getting married?"

"Hell, yes. You've met her sister, Callie, right? She keeps threatening to kill me."

I try to laugh, but I can't. "No, I mean in general. Aren't you worried about your future with Effie?"

"I just want to get this over with. She's been putting me off for a year. I wanted to get married after a month."

"Really?"

"Yeah, man. So what's up with you? You sound funny."

"I ran into my ex out here."

"That's tough," he says. "You okay?"

"No."

Dead air again.

"Elias?"

He sighs. "Listen, I'm terrible on the phone. Hang up and text me. Or better yet, let's get a bite to eat when you come home."

I hang up. So much for my best friend's support. I wish I could talk to Patrick. He'd know what to do. That is, after he kicked my ass for leaving his sister again.

I tear open the gift Burt gave me. It's a leather-bound journal with puppies embossed on the front. I unsnap the strap and read the first page:

Charlie's Field Guide. Keep out, Weiner, or I'll shave your head.

For the next thirty minutes, I read page after page of her innermost thoughts from childhood on.

Every line I read grates a piece of my heart off.

When I reach the part where Patrick told her about the ring, they announce my flight is boarding.

My feet shuffle through the line, barely able to carry my dead weight. I find my window seat and stow my backpack.

In the distance, the setting sun casts a violet hue on the snowy peaks. I crack open the diary and read her last pages. Then I get to this part:

"My family is gone. I don't know what I'd do without Elliott."

Two weeks later

"Elliott is gone. I have no one."

It's like a car just crashed into me. I'm about to walk out on her again. I'm not a stupid twenty-one-year-old kid. I'm a fucking man. A fucking man who needs to grow a pair.

And we're not kids anymore. Everyone has a past. What does it matter if she's a mess? So am I.

Look at Elias and Effie. If they made it, so can we.

Charlie was always there for me growing up, and I need to be there for her now.

My phone vibrates, and a notification from my Buddhist quote-of-the-day app pops up.

"In the end, only three things matter: how much you loved, how gently you lived, and how gracefully you let go of things not meant for you." — Gautama Buddha

---

I grab my phone and dial my parent's house. "Mom? Can you come get me at the airport? I've made a huge mistake."

FIFTY-TWO

Charlie Takes A Bath

Eli's Mixtape: Brandi Carlile, "Raise Hell"

AFTER I TAKE A BATH, I sit in my bathrobe on the couch in front of the fire and watch the snow fall.

Art plops next to me, his mass nearly bouncing me to the floor. For a while, we stare through the window as if it's the most fascinating television program.

"Did he call?" Art asks.

"Who?" I say in an absent-minded voice.

"You really going to play that game with me?"

"No, not yet."

"You okay?"

Actually, it feels like a million needles are lodged in my heart. It's hard to breathe or bleed or live. "I will be."

"Want some cookies and milk?"

"No."

"Want some booze?"

I manage a laugh. "No, I've had enough depressants for the day. I'm just going to be still for a while." And wait for Elliott to come back. Because he's coming back. I know it. Maybe not now, but soon.

Art rubs the back of my neck, and I lean against his shoulder. "Love is hard."

"That it is. But it makes the world glow, sweets, especially you." He lifts my chin with finger. "Don't give up."

I smile through my tears. "I'm thinking about taking a trip to Peru."

"Burt and I took our executives on a company vacation there. Pretty wild. You'd like it. We've got some airline miles if you want to use them before they expire."

"I just may do that." *But not until I hear from Elliott.*

The front door opens, and Burt stomps inside. Our gazes connect, and his mouth twists.

He's not coming back.

Fury shoots through my veins. *Screw him.* I'm going to Machu Picchu.

I turn to Art. "You mentioned I could have your airline miles?"

He stands and ambles over to the front desk. "Let me call my secretary. See if she can't help you out."

"First class, one way." I tell him. "I want to leave New Year's Day."

Screw it. I'll go on an adventure by myself. I don't need anyone else. I've been living on my own for ten years, and I can do it for ten more.

I ask Burt, "How do you feel about watching the boys while I travel around the world?"

"Done," Burt says.

An hour later, I hover my finger above the mouse. My flight is on the screen. Charlotte Sullivan. Seat 1A. I click back and check out the seating map. There are still plenty of seats left. I click "book it," and let out a loud sob.

Then I accept Art's offer for booze and cookies. We play a

game of checkers. I paint my toenails. And I stuff my sorrow into the pit of my belly, where it's been for ten years.

Two hours later, the doorbell rings. Burt pads to the lobby in his bunny slippers and opens the door.

"Welcome back, Bearded Clam."

Air whooshes out of my lungs. *Thank God.*

Elliott nods. "Burt. Art." Eyes a wild blue storm and hair a terrible mess, he doesn't move from the entryway when he greets me. "Hi."

"Hi," I say casually.

"I didn't leave."

"I see that." My pulse is about to jump out of my throat. I swallow and force my attention back to painting my toenails.

Burt and Art get up and leave.

Elliott strolls over and stares at me. "Isn't this the part where you jump into my arms and tongue kiss me?"

"I just painted my nails."

The creases in his forehead deepen.

"Come here, you idiot." I pat the cushion.

My dogs jump on the couch and lick his face. "I missed you guys, too," he tells them, furiously trying to pet all of them at once.

"How was the airport?" I ask.

"Shitty."

"Crowded?"

"Yeah." He pulls an envelope from his back pocket and hands it to me. "Got you these."

I open it slowly. "Hmm. Tickets to Peru. For New Year's Eve." I yawn. "What a coincidence. Same date. Same flight. But I'm in first class. Pity." I stuff them back in the envelope and chuck it at him. "Hope those are refundable."

"They're not." He slips his hand inside mine. "Chicken?"

"Hmm?"

"Are you punishing me?"

"Maybe."

"I'm sorry."

"I know."

"I'm an amateur."

"A total loser."

He tucks me under his arm and lays his cheek atop my head. "I missed you."

"I knew you'd be back. No one can resist my charm and good looks."

"You got that right." His fingers feather sparks up and down my wrist. "Can we kiss and make up now?"

I plop my feet in his lap. "First, I want a foot massage."

The St. James smirk slides up. "You're not going to make this easy on me, are you?"

"Nope. You can kiss your simple life goodbye."

"Screw simple." He rubs a knuckle in the arch of my foot. "I need difficult. I need a challenge. I need you."

"What made you change your mind?"

"I read your journal."

I sit up. "What journal?"

He cracks a grin. "'Elliott is the most beautiful boy alive. He's so nice and wonderful. And I think we should just do it and get it over with.'"

My cheeks burn up. "I never said that."

He wiggles his brows and pulls the journal out of his backpack. "Yes, you did."

"Where did you get that?"

"Burt. Wait until you hear what they did."

I groan. "I don't want to know." I crawl over and get in his lap. "You're such a loser."

His smile presses against mine. "I still have to go back to New York when we get back from our trip."

"Can I come with you?"

"Yep, I'm not leaving you ever again. You're too dangerous on your own."

I hug him so hard he grunts. "I love you."

"Love you, too, Chicken. Oh my God. I can't breathe."
I let go. "I think we should do it."
"I think you're right."

FIFTY-THREE

Eli Reaches The Sun

Survival Tip: When traveling, it's always a good idea to look back at where you were so on the return route, things will be more familiar.

Eli's Mixtape: Donavon Frankenreiter, "Free"

ON THE WAY to South America, Charlie sits in first class and I sit in coach. She visits me in my crappy center seat, only to gloat and wave her free champagne in my face.

When we arrive in Peru, we take off on our five-day hike—twenty-six miles on the Inca trail through lush cloud forests, jungles, and rainbow-colored mountain valleys dotted with wild orchids.

The stone paths, sharp cliffs, soaking rain, and log bridges make for a perilous journey.

Sometimes Charlie sings songs with made-up lyrics. Sometimes I smack her ass to give her a little pick-me-up. "Come on, woman, you're slacking." It's a lie, of course. She never slacks.

And sometimes we hike in silence, awe-struck by the magnificence.

She's always in front of me. I like it better this way. The breathtaking view of her natural beauty against the backdrop of this gorgeous place makes my heart ache with joy.

We walk. We talk. We cheer each other on and laugh. We fall in love again.

At night, we set up camp and dine on yucca, sweet potatoes, and soup with our Peruvian guides around a warm fire. We stare at the stars and plan more adventures. The guides play pan flutes, and it's almost silly how magical it is.

Then, exhausted and electrified, we slip inside our tent and melt together, quietly panting in ecstasy, inhaling our earthy natural scents, and we cling to each other as desperately as we clung to the paths that brought us this far.

"I feel so free," she hums against my skin. "I've never felt like this before."

I stroke her tangled hair. "Me, neither."

Five days later, we arrive at the steps of Machu Picchu, and I suddenly feel deeply religious. There are spirits here. You can feel them in the air.

At the summit, beside Intihuatana, the ritual stone pillar used as a sundial by the ancient ones, Charlie removes three Tupperware containers.

"Jesus, you put your family in Tupperware?"

She shrugs. "It's the lightest thing I could think of. I tried a sandwich baggie, but that just seemed wrong."

I stare at her for a long moment then shake my head.

"I guess we should say a few words?"

"Whatever you want, my love."

Her mouth swishes back and forth then she speaks to the containers. "Hi, Mom. Hi, Dad. Hi, Weiner. I'm sorry it's taken me so long to bring you here." Her voice cracks. "I wasn't ready to let you go. But we all need peace now, and so… here I am. Elliott's here with me. He wants to say a few words."

"I do? Oh, okay. Let's see. I miss you guys. I'm sure you know this, but you were the chosen ones—my preferred family. I'm here with your daughter. She's the sexiest fucking woman I've ever seen—"

Charlie punches my shoulder.

"Ow!" I rub my arm and continue. "Okay, guys, I hope you like it here. It's, I don't know, as close to heaven as we can get, I suppose." I step aside and let Charlie continue.

She inhales a shuddering breath. "Well, I guess it's time. I love you." She lifts the lid off one container.

"Not here," I say. "The wind. You don't want a *Big Lebowski* moment."

"Where should I do it, then?"

"Over there, maybe? By that temple?"

We carry the Tupperware over to the green moss and stand by the edge.

She dumps out the first batch. "Bye, Dad." Then the next. "Bye, Mom." And then the third. "Bye, Weiner." The ashes float on a breeze and swirl down to the cloud cover.

Then she accidentally drops a plastic lid over the edge.

She groans. "We can't just leave that there."

So I scale down the cliff, nearly die on the way down, and retrieve it.

Once that stunt is done, I hold her and smile.

She gives me a soulful kiss. "Thank you."

"Thank *you*, Chicken."

A short while later, we're on our way again, but it's not over, our adventure. It's just the beginning. The beginning of our new story.

FIFTY-FOUR

Charlie Wears Something Ugly

January, Peru

TODAY, Elliott and I got married in a little chapel in Ccaccaccollo, Peru, on our return hike from Machu Picchu.

It was totally spur of the moment. And believe it or not, it was his idea. He told me it was about time he put that ugly ring on my finger.

I've never been so happy to wear something so hideous.

Mine, all mine.

Acknowledgments

Elements of this story really happened. I'll let you guess which ones, but I will tell you this, a lot of readers think I make up a lot of my ad agency stuff. I'm telling you right now, stories like this really exist. Bosses like Skip exist. Clients like this are real. I once had to compete against another agency very much the same way.

I had a lot of help this time. Thanks to my beta readers: Jodie, Julie, and Eileen. They helped make the story much better.

Thanks to my editor, Kiezha, who walked me through plot holes like a fairy godmother.

As always, I'd like to thank my crazy kid and fuzzy dog, for giving me love, even when I'm an asshole on a deadline.

And I'd especially like to thank Irene Oust for loving my books and promoting the hell out of them. Love you, you crazy lady.

About the Author

Nicole Archer's lengthy career as an advertising copywriter not only polished her writing skills—it provided a lifetime of book material. As a single, full-time working mom of a beautiful, brilliant, and horrifically energetic son, she has little time to do much else besides work, write, read, drink wine, and breathe. She's originally from Colorado, but lives in Dallas now. This is her third book.

Newsletter
Website
Facebook page
Facebook group
Twitter
Instagram
Pinterest
Goodreads

Review Me

Hey, Fabulous Reader! Raise your hand if you liked this book? Or better yet, leave a stellar review everywhere. Positive reviews are critical to the survival of new indie authors, and I'd be ever so grateful if you took the time to write one. It helps feed my kid.

Please review me on Amazon, Goodreads, or wherever you purchased your book.

Road-Tripped—Ad Agency Book 1

What's worse than driving across country in a phallic-shaped RV with a coworker you hate? Falling in love with them.

Copywriter, Callie Murphy, has a bad attitude, a vicious tongue, and a serious aversion to Shimura Advertising's resident manwhore, Walker Rhodes. Know where he can stick his good looks and Southern charm? She can think of a few creative places. Avoiding him wouldn't be a problem, except her boss threatens to fire her if she doesn't go along with him on their RV client's cross-country tour.

Walker is sick of his job, tired of women, and in a big old creative rut. The upcoming client road trip is just what he needs to shake things up and rediscover his lost passion. But his plans go south when his partner drops out at the last minute, and Callie, the foul-mouthed tiny terror, takes her place. Unless he can find a way to thaw his icy coworker, he's looking at two months of pure hell.

Buy on Amazon.

Head-Tripped, Ad Agency Book 2

A rock star romance meets Alice in Wonderland.

Effie's a gifted musician and a hot mess.
Elias is the front man in a popular band and hates fame.
They both just want to be normal.
Except there's nothing normal about the way they meet.
And there's definitely nothing normal about the connection they share that weekend.
But he's leaving for his European tour.
And she still has to dig herself out of the hole.
If only they could forget that weekend and go on with their lives.
Or...
He could break all the rules, invite her to play on tour with him, and travel across Europe in a Barbie Disco Bus with a bunch of weirdos.
Normal is boring
Crazy is better.

Or is it?
Buy on Amazon.

Guilt-Tripped—Ad Agency Book 4

Coming soon! Avery Adams' story.

Sign up for my newsletter on nicolearcher.com to get updates.